The HIDDEN Series

Verity Lucia

☦

Book One

HIDDEN

Don't Fear the Unseen

Illustrations by Verity Lucia

ISBN: 979-8-9854383-0-7

Disclaimer

This is a work of fiction. All characters, locations, and businesses are purely products of the author's imagination and are entirely fictitious. Any resemblance to actual people, living or dead, or to businesses, places, or events is completely coincidental.

The author honors the name of our Lord, and is careful not to blaspheme, for character depiction, however, mild language is used on occasion in this book. The full spelling of the language is not written out but is instead filled in with asterisk characters.
The author does not condone the desecration of relics or holy items of any kind.

This book contains elements of fictional fantasy but is written with the intent to illustrate the truth and tenets of the Christian faith. Every effort was made to make clear what is truth and what is fiction. Artistic license was taken to share the information in an accurate yet interesting and educational manner.

Reference materials were used in the creation of this book and were cited with care. We greatly respect and admire the other works that are quoted in this material and hope that those source authors are not offended at the use within this work of fiction. Please contact the author directly if there are any concerns. Thank you.

For my daughter, Aliya, without whose enthusiasm this book would not have taken shape. You are an inspiration to me. Thank you for all the special ways you contributed to this novel along the way.
I love you so much.

Table of Contents

✝

Book One

HIDDEN

Don't Fear the Unseen

This is Clare's story.

"A wicked person desires the catch of evil people, but the root of the righteous will bear fruit. By the sin of their lips the wicked are ensnared, but the just escape from a tight spot."
Proverbs 12:13

1

Friday

BEEP BEEP BEEP...........BEEP BEEP BEEP...........

"Oh, crap! No, I did not just sleep through my alarm again!" Clare flew out of bed, throwing on the first clothes she saw on her floor. Stumbling down the stairs, the scent of burnt toast filled her nose as her thoughts raced.

Clare's little brother, James, sat at the kitchen counter making disgusted faces at his plate of egg whites and blackened bread while her father scraped furiously at the black crust with a butter knife.

"It's fine, James. I'll put some jelly on it, and you won't even taste it. Whoa, whoa, whoa, young lady! You are not leaving the house wearing that," her father said sternly to Clare as she rushed into the kitchen.

"Oh, you've got to be kidding me, Dad! I'm already late!"

"End of discussion. Go back upstairs and change that shirt."

"UGGGHHHHHHH!"

As Clare headed back to her room, she had already resolved to sneak her skimpy tank top into her backpack. She exchanged it for a modest T-shirt and sweater. This would get her past her overbearing father and to school, where she could change in the bathroom between classes. She would have to wear what she had on for first period.

While riding her bike to school, she passed the old, abandoned paper mill—crumbling smokestacks precariously still standing. The roads were steaming from the fresh rain on the

3

hot tarmac. *That place gives me the creeps,* Clare thought as she flew past.

She raced down the residential streets, riding the yellow centerline, swerving swiftly up onto the sidewalks, and cutting through the corners of the neighborhood's freshly trimmed lawns. Finally arriving at the school's parking lot, she quickly locked her bike up next to a bench by the football field and ran as fast as she could into the building.

The halls were empty.

She cringed as she realized just how late she was, already dreading the dozens of judgmental eyes that would soon be on her.

She crept into class, trying not to be noticed, and slipped into her seat. She successfully avoided eye contact by staring vaguely out of the closest window.

The drone of Ms. Clopher's voice rambling on about Greek and Latin root words was enough to make anyone stop listening. It took what seemed like forever for the first-period bell to ring. As it did, Clare was the first one out the door.

She quickly changed in the bathroom before her friends noticed what she had been wearing.

"Hey, Clare!" Nikki's voice cut through the deafening noise of clanging lockers and cackling laughter. Most of the Cheer team was huddled together near the base of the second-floor staircase—Nikki Thacker towering over them, not in height but status. They all looked so cool and...coordinated. Clare often wondered if they texted each other every morning to determine what the day's outfits would be.

Clare was one of the only girls in the group *not* on the Cheer team and often felt like an outsider—an imposter even. *She* wasn't included in any morning group text...

What had they just been laughing about? Were they whispering about me? Being around Nikki seemed to cause insecurities to ooze from Clare's skin, but it felt so great to be part of the group when things were good.

"Did you hear about the party that Finn and Colton are throwing tonight down at the sandbar?" Nikki said as she approached Clare. "It's gonna be lit. Colton swiped a bottle of his old man's Jim Beam."

"...I'm down," Clare replied as she pulled books out of her locker.

"Don't be a Karen. If you flake on me again like you did last weekend, I'm going to be ticked."

"C'mon, Clare. This may be the last warm weekend we'll get," Elise cajoled.

"All right, I'll be there," Clare replied, grabbing her last book out and slamming her locker.

Just then, their attention shifted. Clare shrunk inside herself. Her old friend, Caitlin, was coming down the hall. Some harsh words had created a chasm in the relationship. The fight left a void that now felt too great to repair. These days Caitlin couldn't make it from one class to the next without being harassed by Nikki and her crew. Clare wondered why she felt such a need to be accepted by Nik. It was probably the way everyone looked at the girl. Like she mattered. Like she had the power to make or break a person. If you were in with Nikki, you were in with the whole school.

"Oh no," Clare whispered under her breath.

Elise, Nikki's personal henchman, was moving to strike. She caught Caitlin's dragging shoelaces just in time to send her flying. Her books went sprawling across the faded checkered floor.

"Ten points for loser down!" Nikki chuckled while smacking hands with Elise.

Clare moved ever so slightly in Caitlin's direction but quickly thought better of it. She wanted to help, but there was nothing worse than being on Nikki's bad side. As bad as she felt for Caitlin, it just wasn't worth it.

Caitlin scooped up her books and stared up at Clare. Their eyes met briefly. A heavy feeling of guilt landed in Clare's gut. Lunch couldn't come soon enough. *Even bland, pasty mac and cheese would be better than this sickening feeling in my stomach.*

Bells rang. Classes came and went. The lunchroom was filled with starving students, each table categorized by class—by subclass that is—geeks at one and jocks at another. Nikki's table was in the back corner by the window. Clare positioned herself in the last seat against the wall. Clare could see straight down the aisle from this angle with a perfect view of the Christian table. Everyone knew they were Bible lovers because they always prayed before they ate. Nikki loved this. She thought it was hysterical. Clare loved this perspective for a different reason. His name was Noah.

She couldn't not look at him.

There was just something about him that was different from all the rest. Was it his smile? Or his serious, brown eyes? Maybe it was his walk—confident—like he didn't even care what people thought.

"Wake up, Clare Bear!" Nikki jabbed, snapping her fingers in front of Clare's face. "You've been staring at that Bible-thumping hottie for like ten minutes now. If you want him, why don't you just walk up there and make it happen? Or..." She stood up, immediately commanding the table's attention. "Or I could do it for you." She took a step in that direction. As she did, Noah glanced up at her.

"No, no, no, Nikki, I'm good. I was just zoning out," Clare said, shrinking slightly.

"Really? Because d***, girl, you're lookin' thirsty."

"So, Nik!" Elise interjected, grabbing Nikki's left arm and pulling her down beside her. "I was thinking, since my step-dad moved out, my mom's been working the night shift, so you could totally sleep at my place next week."

Clare always wondered why the most popular girl in school, with the most enviable house in town—I'm talking pool, pool house, and pool boy level enviable—would make a habit of crashing anywhere but her own home, but she did.

"Don't be stupid," Nikki replied. "Why would I want to stay at your mom's when I could crash at Colton's?" She leaned over and slid her hand into the back jean pocket of the athletic, dusty-haired boy next to her.

"Sorry, Nikki. I just thought it would be fun," Elise stammered, apparently feeling insecure. Nikki had a way of making even the most confident people feel tiny and insignificant.

"What's gonna be fun is the rager we're throwing tonight. Am I right?" Nikki pivoted to knock elbows with a dark-haired girl to her left and a skinny boy who sat opposite her.

Clare observed the way everyone's eyes were on Nikki as she spoke. *Look at her*, Clare thought. *How is it that even her hair seems to obey her commands?* Clare couldn't recall a moment when it had ever looked out of place.

Not only was she gorgeous and blond, but she was practically school royalty. Nikki was captain of the Cheer squad, making her de facto leader of all of the most popular girls in school. And although she didn't really seem to actively participate in much else—other than parties and boys, that is—her older brother, Jason Thacker, had been quarterback of the Jefferson High Varsity football team. The team won the title two years in a row with Jason as captain before the Georgia Bulldogs recruited him, and everyone knows they're the best college football team there ever was.

And on top of that, Nikki's younger brother, Anthony, appeared to be following in his celebrated brother's footsteps. Although Anthony was only a freshman, the coaches were already allowing him to play varsity.

Cash was another thing that set Nikki's family apart. They were custom 'Jimmy Choo sneakers' rich. In a year of allowances, what

Clare could save wouldn't buy her even one of Nikki's everyday outfits. Apparently, her father was loaded. Who knew a bank manager had such a lush salary.

As the bell rang, Nikki stood up, and the rest of her crowd followed in unison, grabbing their designer backpacks. They strutted together out of the lunchroom, laughing at their inside jokes.

If your grades weren't great, and your looks weren't special, just sitting at the right table with the right people made you someone.

✝

"No, Mom. I don't have any homework," Clare lied. Back at home, the line between lies and truth felt so fluid lately. *What difference does it make anyway? People only hear what they want to hear. And as long as things work out my way, who cares.*

"Mom," Clare began, innocently sweeping her hair out of her eyes and tossing it over her shoulder, "Caitlin asked if I could come over

13

tonight. She rented some movies, and her mom promised to bring home some of the good popcorn from the cinema."

"I guess that'd be all right," her mom replied, "but you can't stay the night. We're all getting up early to get everything ready for the garage sale."

"Yeah, no problem. Thanks, Mom."

"Just be home by 10:30, okay?"

Clare double-stepped it up the stairs to her room before her mom had a chance to ask any more questions.

Her bedroom was much like the rest of her home—casual and comfortable, cluttered with beloved knick-knacks and souvenirs from family trips. She stepped over yesterday's clothing, still on the beige, carpeted floor, and crossed the room to study her face in her dresser-top mirror.

How much makeup can I get away with? Ugh, is that a zit?!

No, just another stupid freckle appearing as if by magic on the end of her nose.

Clare noticed every new freckle, mole, pimple, and hair these days. She spent almost as much time staring at her reflection as scrolling through TikTok and checking her Instagram page.

Every ping and phantom vibration had her reaching for her phone, swiping intently to verify that followers had increased and that her friend list hadn't decreased. She was careful to 'like' appropriately and 'share' only the vetted cool. She mostly re-posted whatever Nikki or Elise shared. The less she had to think about it, the better.

What Clare spent the most time doing on her social apps wasn't precisely 'social' in nature. She spent hours losing herself in the world of crafted selfies. She lost days of her life this way.

How is it that everyone had a more exciting life than her? Better vacations, cuter boyfriends, plumper lips. Even the lighting was better in their photos. It's like God shone on them, and she was living in the gray leftovers of the social world. Maybe she had done something to deserve it.

Her pale complexion and dull auburn hair had never earned her much attention—positive attention anyway. Blond. That's what I'll do. I'll just get a box of dye from the drugstore next time I ride into town.

Clare spent the following couple of hours primping while her phone blew up with texts about tonight's party. "It's gonna be lit," Clare repeated, half mockingly, half nervously.

She meticulously chose her outfit while watching YouTube videos to ensure she was applying her eyeshadow with proper technique. Then she studied Elise's Instagram page for the latest post on fashion do's and don'ts, after which she selected the tightest pair of high-waisted jeans in her closet, before pairing it with a low-cut teal crop top that showed just the right amount of torso. She threw a modest polo over it and slid a crimson lipstick into her back pocket.

Heading out, she paused at the door before backtracking to tear a sample of Vera Whoever's Princess perfume out of a copy of Teen Vogue. She stuck it snugly next to the lipstick.

After all, if she didn't have a signature scent, who was she anyway?

✝

The blaring music projecting from Finn's battered Jeep Wrangler was not subtle, to say the least. How the cops had not already shown up had to be a minor miracle. She rode her matte black road bike down the gravel road to join the group.

Nikki wasn't kidding. Everyone who was anyone at Jefferson High was there. "Clare!" Elise's squeal pierced through the noise. "I can't believe you actually came!" Elise's bubbly giggle and unusually bright smile were evidence that she had clearly been down here for a while already, the thick smell of booze radiating off her skin as she hung with her arms strewn around Finn's neck.

"C'mon! Take a swig!" She handed Clare the nearly empty bottle of whiskey. Clare put it to her lips and slugged it back, the warm, bitter taste causing her to choke. She felt the burn in her throat and her eyes began to water.

"Hahaha!" Elise cackled. "Good, right?" She winked at Clare, grabbed Finn by the wrist, and led him forcefully down to the water's edge.

Clare stepped from the cold, dark periphery of the woods and joined the party. The warmth of the alcohol and the glow of the firelight made her feel that she was on the edge of something ...something exciting....something forbidden.

Bottles passed from hand to hand, hand to lips, and back again.

The night air swirled with laughter and shouts.

Hours passed.

Clare's thoughts blurred together as she stumbled across the rocky ground to the river shore. She sat upright, staring into the night sky.

The stars seem to be moving on their own.

This made her suddenly uneasy.

She became aware of the fuzz in her brain.

What am I doing? How am I going to get home? She pressed her cool palms into her forehead.

She gazed out at the glistening water, mesmerized by the reflection of the moonlight. She struggled to straighten out her thoughts but found that she couldn't.

"Hey, girl," a stocky blond boy said as he slid swiftly and assertively beside her. "Saw you over here all alone. Thought you could use some company." He then squared his shoulders to hers, took her chin, turned her face to his, and kissed her before Clare could realize what was going on.

"Stop it!" she shouted while trying to stand up.

"C'mon, babe, you know you want to." He grasped her wrists, pulling her forcefully back down next to him.

"No, really. I DON'T." At this, she kicked him hard in the shin and scrambled back up the bank.

Where was her bike?

It had to be so late.

She ran, pushing through a group of kids laughing in a cloud of smoke. There was Nikki, making out with Colton, her legs hanging out of his dad's brand new Dodge Charger. She didn't even notice Clare making her way towards the road.

There!

My bike!

Clare picked it up to get on, pushed the pedal once, and toppled down, knocking her knee into a projecting rock. Her jeans ripped, and a trickle of blood began to form.

She straightened the bike out again, focusing her eyes ahead of her with increased alertness, and took off. The cold wind was sobering. She was thirsty—really thirsty, actually. *I have to get home.* She sped down the gravel road back towards town.

As she rode those few miles towards home, the night air grew cool after the warm day, and fog rose from the damp pavement. Her mind was confused, and her vision now blurred.

She rode in silence, hearing only the smooth hum of the rubber bike tires on the road and the sharp *click click click click* of the chain going around the sprocket as she glided down the road.

No crickets.

No birds.

Then her bike bumped, and she felt the pavement turn to gravel under her tires.

Startled, Clare slowed her bike to a stop and looked around. *I don't remember coming through here on my way down,* Clare thought as she wiped the sweat from her eyes.

Crap, I must've taken a wrong turn.

Her heart rate increased, and she felt sweat permeate her palms.

She turned her head to the left.

And then the right.

And then up.

Rusting smokestacks were towering over her with their eerily looming forms. From this vantage point, she couldn't even see the tops, disguised as they were in a haze.

She was in the abandoned yard of the old paper mill.

However, what was more disconcerting than the towering smokestacks was the infinite black darkness ahead of her. One of the enormous gray buildings had been partially demolished to extract some of the remaining valuable equipment, leaving a massive wound in the steely facade.

The distant street lights cast a faint orange glow but could not penetrate the abyss of the ominous gash. Chills ran over Clare's arms as she felt the presence of the immense darkness.

She peered into it, squinting her eyes.

The air felt heavy, and the inky darkness appeared almost touchable. She stretched one hand out towards the blackness.

Her thoughts were cut short.

A gust of wind burst forth from the cavern. She sucked in fast—finding it hard to breathe. The tingling chills that had started at her arms ran up her neck and down to her feet.

She edged forward slowly, her feet nudging the pedals.

A crunch stopped her short. Clare glanced down at her front bicycle tire. There, on the dusty gray gravel, something shimmered in the darkness. *What in the...* Clare looked down and squinted.

She bent down and picked up a brassy pair of Aviator sunglasses. Then she held them up to her face and studied them briefly, running her thumb across a tiny logo on the upper corner of the lens. The symbol was strange—two inverted V's or maybe two X's? It was difficult to say. As she held them up to her face, the moonlight glinted off of them.

Just then, a deafening howl rang out from the heart of the fortress of buildings!

The shock knocked Clare backward, shaking her from her brain haze and setting her back on course. Clare realized her absolute aloneness, her utter vulnerability, and took off with fierce speed in the direction of the warm orange street lights.

She wove through the empty but familiar streets, arriving back in her driveway as she heard the nearby church bells strike twelve. As she dropped her bike on the dewy lawn and ran around to the side door, fumbling with her house key, the door swung open; her parents' silhouettes were distinct in the doorway.

✝

"Where have you been?" Clare's father's booming voice reverberated through the kitchen.

Clare stood, silent. She was sure they picked up on the scent of liquor and cigarettes the moment the door cracked open.

"Clare, I can't understand—" her mother began.

"Caitlin wanted me to stay late to study. She—"

"Don't even start. I called over there and spoke with Mrs. Hill. You weren't there. You never planned to be there. She said you and Caitlin haven't spoken for months. What's going on with you lately, Clare? I know you know the difference between right and wrong. We love you. We love you so much, in fact, that we can't allow you to continue to make these choices. And, therefore... you're grounded."

"Mom! C'mon!" Clare protested.

"It's best if you go to bed now. We can talk about this more in the morning."

"You never would have treated Ethan this way!"

"What did you just say—if I ever hear you talk about your brother—GO TO YOUR ROOM!"

"Mom?" A small voice came from around the corner. It was James.

"James, honey, what are you doing up?" Clare's Mom scooped up the sweet, three-year-old boy, whispering soft words to him as she carried him back to his room.

Clare's head hung. The stairs to her room had never before felt so steep.

"Watch carefully then how you live, not as foolish persons but as wise, making the most of the opportunity, because the days are evil."
Ephesians 5:15-16

2
Saturday

The ache—the pounding—the pressure in Clare's head was too much. The rays of sun coming in through her bedroom window were too bright. A chatter echoed up the stairs from the kitchen. Her parents—no doubt, plotting her demise. Clare shrugged on her robe and trudged downstairs.

No point putting off the inevitable. Besides, the smell of bacon and pancakes and the promise of Tylenol were enough to draw even a corpse from its grave.

"Sit down, Clare." Her father gestured toward a stool at the end of the kitchen island. He poured her a glass of orange juice and set a plate of pancakes and bacon in front of her.

"Clare," her mom began, "I'd just like to start by apologizing for losing my temper with you last night. While using your brother's memory to make excuses for yourself is absolutely unacceptable, I shouldn't have raised my voice at you like I did. That being said, I never want to hear you speak of Ethan like that again. We loved him dearly, just as we love you. I miss him every day of my life, and I know you do too. I also realize how difficult things have been for you this past year, but it doesn't justify what you are doing—getting drunk with these people you call friends...lying to us. It's not going to bring him back. It's hard to make sense of it all. But we have to trust in God's plan."

Clare shrugged her shoulders and set down her fork.

A tear dropped from her eye and landed on her plate, creating a tiny, iridescent pool next to her bacon. "Mom...I hate it..." she began softly and then shook her head. "It's not fair! Ethan was good! He did everything right! And look at what happened to him! Hit by some drunk! How does that make sense?! What kind of God does that?!" Clare stood up, shoved her plate forward, and ran up the carpeted stairs to her bedroom, tears streaming down her face.

She knelt on her bed, head bowed towards her worn wooden headboard. She gripped the hand-sewn comforter and pulled it up to her watery eyes. "Nothing makes sense anymore," Clare said, her hushed voice barely audible even to herself. She tensed her arms and legs as if she could will herself out of existence.

Her bedroom walls were closing in on her.

She began to sweat.

"I can't...I can't breathe...I have to get out of here." Urgent and confused thoughts rushed through her head. She stood up, got dressed hastily, and grabbed her backpack, quickly shoving things into it, not knowing exactly for what she was packing.

She pulled up on the sash of her bedroom window, careful not to make too much noise. She maneuvered nimbly out onto the porch roof and down a nearby tree branch, where she was able to slide down to a safe jumping height.

Once down on the ground, she quickly jogged to the sidewalk. She glanced back at her picturesque, historic home before cautiously making her way around the corner and out of sight.

She walked mindlessly, weaving her way among the city streets. She looked around, breathing deeply to take in the comforting, earthy autumn air.

A young boy laughed as he threw a ball to his dog in his picket-fenced yard. The next block down, a man hugged a young woman—probably his daughter, home from college, overflowing laundry bag in tow.

Clare stared at them in wonder. *It's so strange when someone you love dies—how for you the world seems to stop. But for everyone else, it keeps turning. Everyone is seeing in color while I'm living in a world of stale black and white.*

Clare gradually made her way to a nearby boat landing—a place she frequently visited when she needed to think. Somehow being near the water always helped to clear her mind.

She strolled to the end of the dock. Her hollow-sounding footsteps echoed below the deck planks as she sat down cross-legged and gazed up into the cloudless sky. This afternoon, there were no boats on the river. Only the reflection of the just-turning maple trees rippled across the water.

Clare sat motionless, unfeeling. Her feet dangled off the side of the dock. Her thoughts suspended in unknowns.

She was
waiting for
something.

Some kind of
sign.

Some kind of
reassurance.

She waited
for what felt
like hours, her
skin turning

pink from the hot summer sun.

Clare lowered her head, then jumped abruptly to her feet, shoulders back and chin raised towards the sky. "Do you even exist?!" she shouted up at the clear blue heavens, her voice cold and piercing. "No good God would let my brother die! How could you do this to me and my family?!" Clare held her breath and listened for an answer...

But all she heard were screeching blue jays and the rippling sound of the water hitting against the boat landing.

She looked down, digging for her composure, but instead felt her chest tighten and warm tears flood her eyes. Feeling lost and desperate, she slumped back down on the dock and reached for her phone.

A group text. "Bored as crap. Where y'all at?"

Her phone vibrated almost instantly. "Hey, girl! Spent the night at Colton's dad's cabin. Get your @$$ down here!" blinked across her screen.

Clare stood up.

Her body felt heavy.

She wiped the tears from her eyes, uprighted her bike, and texted Elise that she was on her way.

Before riding off, she dug into her bag and put on the sunglasses she had found the night before. They would work well to cover her puffy, bloodshot eyes. If Nikki saw that she'd been crying, she would never hear the end of it.

She rode along the long and winding river road, down the hill below the dam where the river opened up to an expansive, glittering lake. Chicago was only a couple hours away, and Heron Lake was the kind of place that city dwellers referred to as 'up north.' Most of the homes that dotted the shore weren't for full-time use. During the week, the lake was almost desolate but would be cluttered with speed boats and water skiers on the weekends.

After a mile or so, Clare approached the stately log cabin. She could hear the roaring engines of racing Jet Skis and the laughing voices of Nikki and Elise. She glided her bike along the gravel drive and coasted down the hill to join the girls in the backyard.

She glanced up and let out a horrifying shriek as she lost control of her bike and slid out onto her stomach on the grass. She cringed with pain and fright. There, hovering above the sunbathing girls, were two HUGE, dark forms with gruesome, scabby, ghostly faces!

Clare shook her head while getting herself to her feet and whipped off her glasses to get a better look but saw nothing but the dumbfounded expression on Elise's face.

"What the h***?!" Nikki shouted at Clare, both arms raised in the air.

"I just saw...I just saw...." Clare stammered. She put the glasses back on and fell backward onto her butt in the grass.

There they were again!

Dark shadowy creatures were whispering into the girls' ears!

Two more creatures were flying swiftly alongside the speeding Jet Skis as if they were riding sidecar. As she looked closer, she saw that they had deformed, grotesque expressions—not at all human-like, but almost like murderous apes with fangs and black pits for eyes.

Their crippled, distorted fingers gestured wildly at the girls. Clare ripped the glasses off her face and scrambled back onto her bike. She had to get out of there! She pushed the resisting pedals hard as she glanced back to see Nikki and Elise standing incredulously, watching her go.

She had never ridden home so fast; the trees whipped past her as if she were riding in a speeding car. A red convertible flew through an intersection, narrowly missing her as she sped through town, ignoring the stoplights.

The moment she got home, she threw her bike to the ground and climbed back up the tree, through her window, into the safety of her bedroom.

"What did I just see?" Clare mumbled as her chest heaved with gasping breaths. *I must have gotten too much sun. Or maybe I did drink way too much last night...yeah, that must be it,* she thought as she paced back and forth, *either that or...or there's something really weird going on with these glasses...*

She tugged the hairband out from her ponytail, letting her tousled locks fall to her shoulders as she jogged across the room to her desk, slamming open her laptop.

Her head hovered over the keyboard as she furiously punched the keys, inserting words like 'enchanted sunglasses' and 'am I hallucinating' into the search bar.

The only thing that came up was a dumb children's book about magic glasses on a creepy cat and about a dozen medical reasons for spontaneous hallucinations.

But what were those creatures? How could I see them? Why could I see them when I was wearing sunglasses but not when I took them off? Why were they so interested in my friends? Is it possible they could have followed me home? Is there one with me right now!?

Clare shivered.

She pulled the glasses from her backpack and carefully placed them into her dresser drawer. *Maybe it was just bad booze, or maybe they are magic or something...either way...it's best if they stay here for now.*

Clare slid the drawer shut.

She collapsed on her bed and covered her head with her blanket.

Knock, knock, knock. "Honey, dinner's ready. You've been in there all day. Please come and join us," her mom's muffled voice called from the other side of the door.

Clare's mom and dad chatted lightly about their day at the dinner table. Thankfully, it seemed no one had noticed she had gone missing earlier. *Maybe there are miracles after all.* Clare sat there, quietly pushing food around on her plate.

"Are you going to eat that?" James asked, gazing at her sweetly. Clare just shook her head.

James smiled and replied, "I know. Meatloaf is pretty 'scusting."

Clare smiled back.

✝

The lunchroom was crowded with hungry students. Every seat was filled. Row upon row of tables was loaded with row upon row of trays.

Clare sat alone at a table with eleven other empty seats.

She had no tray—no food at all.

She became aware of an overwhelming odor of rotting garbage. Nauseous yet starving, she looked around her and noticed everyone was eating, but no one was talking. The only sound she heard was the noise of chips—crunching.

Everyone was eating the same food—at the same time. Rhythmically raising fists full of broken potato chips to their ravenous mouths, chewing mechanically. Staring blankly.

Hands grabbed.

Fists raised.

Chewing, chewing, chewing, chewing.

Hands grabbed.

Fists raised.

Chewing, chewing, chewing, chewing.

Clare stood up, a sense of dread coming over her. Then, suddenly, the chewing STOPPED. Each of the hundreds of heads in the vast room spun around to glare at her, some of them rotating a full 180 degrees.

Terrified, she turned to run but found her feet wouldn't budge. They were nailed to the floor.

Move, move, MOVE!

A ring of smoke was encroaching on her from all sides. From out of the haze, black, tar-covered hands were reaching. Reaching for HER!

What did they want with her?! And then a piercing scream! It was the dark forms with their hysterical ape-like faces!

Then...WHITE.

Clare shot upright in her bed, dripping with sweat. It was a dream. "It was only a dream," she reassured herself.

It was only a dream, wasn't it?

"Blessed are the merciful, for they will be shown mercy."
Matthew 5:7

3
Sunday

"Whoever isn't in the car in five minutes doesn't get a donut after!" Clare's father shouted into the house from the garage. Sunday was always the tensest morning of the week. For some reason, getting all four of them out of the house and to church on time seemed like an impossible task and brought out the worst in all of them.

"Give me my shoe, James!" Clare yelled at her little brother, who was jumping back and forth on the living room sofa with a black dress shoe in one hand and a half-eaten banana in the other, looking unmistakably like an irritating little monkey.

Clare's mother plucked both items from the boy's hands, tossing the browning banana into the trash with one hand and the shoe to her daughter with the other. "all right, that's enough from both of you," she said sternly. Get in the car. We're going to be late."

"It's not like Father will know," Clare said snarkily. She pictured Father Mike with his dark sunglasses and cane. He never went anywhere without his gigantic pony of a dog—a wolfhound named Charlie. The bishop didn't much like having a dog in the church, but they made an exception for the blind pastor.

"God sees all, dear," her mother responded while giving Clare a 'don't give me that attitude, young lady' look.

They pulled up to St. Anne's, parking on the street because there was no room in the lot.

The family hustled towards the imposing stone facade, yanking open the heavy, oak doors. There was no way to slip in without being noticed. The doors were centrally located, right on the middle aisle, and even if you walked with the grace of a ballet dancer, the click of your shoes could still be heard echoing through the great space.

The entire congregation was standing. Then, as if on cue, everyone sat down.

"Oh, good," Clare's mom murmured. "We haven't missed the readings." One by one, they knelt, and each sidestepped into a pew beside an elderly couple. Deacon Schmitt was at the pulpit. He was reading from the first book of Peter. His voice resounded through the church in a way that small children even sometimes mistook for the voice of God Himself.

Clare wasn't paying attention to his words today, though. She was distracted. Her eyes flitted from one person to the next, picking up on every mismatched outfit and out-of-date hairstyle.

Then she saw him. Noah.

He was standing tall, shoulders back with the missalette open. He was reading along. It was then that Deacon's words caught her attention, "Be sober, be watchful. Your adversary, the devil, prowls around like a roaring lion, seeking someone to devour."

What did he just say? What the heck does that mean?

He continued, "Resist him, firm in your faith, knowing that the same experience of suffering is required of your brotherhood throughout the world. And after you have suffered a little while, the God of all grace, who has called you to his eternal glory in Christ, will himself restore, establish, and strengthen you. To him be the dominion for ever and ever. Amen. The word of the Lord."

And the congregation responded in unison, "Thanks be to God."

Everyone stood at once.

Together, the congregation sang the Alleluia, a song of praise to God. Then, Deacon read the Gospel, and as Father Mike moved slowly to the pulpit to give the homily, Clare's thoughts swirled in her head. *Did he just say that there are creatures here on earth that want to* destroy us? He can't be serious, right? I mean, it's not like the Bible is literal...is it?

Father Mike began, "Some of you have been told that there is no such thing as evil. The world would have us believe that there is no right and wrong, that there is only what is right for me and what is wrong for me. That there is no truth. No black and white, but only shades of gray. It's all relative, right? Wrong. Truth can be known. And there is right and wrong and good and evil. You only have to look around to see it. The evidence is everywhere. Wars, cruelty, sacrifice, and kindness. We are in a spiritual battle—right now. Does it sound like I'm being overly dramatic? Was Jesus being overly dramatic when he said in Luke 10:18, 'I saw Satan fall like lightning from heaven'? He says this to prepare us—to make us aware! But do not fear. Do not despair! The Lord provided us with tools to ready ourselves and weapons of spiritual warfare to defend ourselves. He left us this prayer in Luke 11:2-4, 'When you pray, say: Father, hallowed be your name. Your kingdom come. Give us each day our daily bread and forgive us our sins, for we ourselves forgive everyone who is indebted to us; and lead us not into temptation.'

"Temptation." He paused. "Temptation is not itself a sin but leads us to it. It comes from within us and outside ourselves—from our own human weakness *and* from the evil one and his army. Are you prepared to do battle with the dark forces that assail you? Are you covered in the armor of God? Let us pray together; Saint Michael, the Archangel, defend us in battle, be our protection against the wickedness and snares of the devil. May God rebuke him, we humbly pray, and do thou, oh Prince of the Heavenly Host, by the power of God, cast into hell Satan and all the evil spirits who prowl about the world seeking the ruin of souls. Amen."

Clare had heard the prayer before, but today, the booming, united voices imploring God to save them from evil took on new meaning. Visions of last night's nightmare filled her mind. She shuddered. She glanced again at Noah, who was now kneeling, his eyes closed, head lowered in prayer.

Clare, too, closed her eyes, and whispered three words, "God, help me."

✝

The family loaded into the car and headed home after Mass. James was eager to get back to work at the 'cash register' with his sister. The community garage sale was a semi-holiday for the Thomsons. They prepared for it for weeks just to have it over in a weekend. Today was Clare's and James' turn at the checkout table.

When they arrived home, Clare ran to her room, changed into jeans and a hoodie, and opened her desk drawer. She could see her face reflected back in the lenses of the mysterious glasses.

"Clare! Hurry up!" her mom's voice shouted from down the hall, "There are already shoppers here!" Clare stuck the glasses in her pocket and joined her family outside. Several older ladies were milling about between the boxes filled to the brim with old clothes, Christmas china, tablecloths, and the like.

Clare sat down in the garage with her feet propped up on the folding card table, a bag of small change next to her sneakered feet. She reached into her back pocket and pulled out her phone, quickly typing 'aviators' into the Pinterest search bar. She began swiftly scrolling through the feed, trying to find a matching image of the strange glasses she now possessed.

Her mother's voice bellowed from behind her, "I don't think so. It's screen-free Sunday, young lady." Her mom plucked the cell from her daughter's hands.

Screen-free Sunday had become a tradition in

the Thomson family. Instead of watching TV or playing on their phones, they were supposed to bond by playing board games or whatever. Outwardly, Clare hated the idea of mushy family togetherness, but secretly the memories of her and Ethan playing UNO at the dinner table were some of her most cherished times.

Everything seemed so simple then.

Frustrated, she shoved her empty, phoneless hands into her hoodie pocket. She took the glasses between her thumb and forefinger, spinning them in the sunlight.

Just then, two young boys started bickering. Each had their hands on the same GameBoy console, hovering and pulling tug-of-war style over the top of an antique tea set.

"Whoa, whoa, whoa! Boys!" Clare snapped as she rose to break up the tussle. "Why don't you check out this Nintendo Switch over here? See, you can each have one. No need to fight." Clare bent over to pick her brother's old game system out of a cardboard box, handing it to the taller of the two boys.

A twinge of regret rushed through her.

Selling Ethan's old things made it so...official.

She turned back towards the table. A young, dark-haired girl was standing there. Was she waiting to check out? No, it was Caitlin. What did she have in her hands? She held Clare's sunglasses, appearing to study the logo laminated to the lens.

Clare lunged forward. "Stop it!" she shouted as she yanked the sunglasses out of Caitlin's hands.

Caitlin flinched at the unexpected confrontation. "I was just... I'm sorry..." Caitlin stammered while shaking her head.

She brushed her dark curls back from her sullen face and turned to leave.

"Caitlin—I'm—" Clare interjected, trying to repair her misstep.

"Mom, I'm ready to go," Caitlin said as she moved to her mother's side, not even glancing back before leaving.

Clare's mom had been watching. She moved to her daughter's side, pulling her in for a half-hug. "I saw the Hills at church this morning." She explained, "I invited them over for the garage sale today. I thought you and Caitlin could talk—work things out."

"It's not that simple, Mom." Clare shrugged off her mother's affection. "It's just not that simple."

That evening passed as every recent Sunday night did—quiet and slow over a game of mandatory cards, Ethan's empty seat too loud to ignore.

"If the world hates you, realize that it hated me first."
John 15:18

4

Monday

Waking early enough to get to school with plenty of time to spare, Clare sat perched on the end of her bed, holding the aviators in both hands together as if they were a freshly hatched chick.

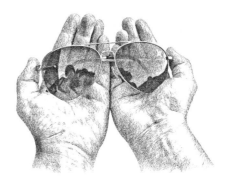

She hadn't been able to think of much else since they had come into her life.

Where did they come from?

How do they work?

Her curiosity consumed her. Maybe she was going crazy. Or perhaps these sunglasses did somehow make visible to her some invisible world.

She had to know more. See more.

She resolved to put them on when she got to school to see if those creatures were there again with Nikki and the group.

Outside the school doors, Clare reached into her front backpack pocket, pulled out the glasses, and pushed them over her ears, settling them comfortably on her delicate face. She yanked both double doors open and stepped in assertively.

Nothing could have prepared her for what she saw. There were dozens of ghostly dark forms. Those she expected to see. But among them and the bustling groups of students were also fiery forms of light, so bright she found them difficult to look at and, so, difficult to discern.

She walked towards one of them, hoping to get a better look. She reached out towards it, expecting to sense heat of some kind. Just then, the glasses were snatched off her face.

"What, you think you look cool or something? Sunglasses inside, seriously?! What was that on Saturday, Clare? Screaming on the lawn like some kind of freak?!" Nikki was cruel and taunting in her tone. She dangled the glasses over Clare's head before flinging them into an oversized plastic garbage bin. She smirked at Clare and then turned to saunter down the hall while gesturing for Elise and Colton to follow.

Clare assumed things would be awkward today with the girls, but she couldn't have anticipated this level of rejection. She turned and pressed her forehead into the ugly, orange lockers as heat flooded her cheeks. She felt a touch on her shoulder.

"I just saw what happened," Noah said tenderly. "Are you okay?"

Saying nothing, Clare turned away from Noah and ran, sobbing, down the hall and out the large gray exit doors.

She frantically unlocked her bike from the rusty rack. She rode straight home, barging through the front door, ignoring her mother, who was sitting on the floor with her little brother playing with Legos.

She charged straight up to her bedroom and slammed the door behind her before burying her head under her pillow.

Half-sobbing, half-screaming, she let out a guttural sound. "Why?! Why did I ever pick up those stupid sunglasses?! Why is this happening to me?!"

"What on earth is going on? Why are you not at school right now?" Clare's mom demanded answers as she burst into Clare's room unannounced.

Clare looked up, tears streaming down her face. Her mother's face softened.

"Oh, honey, what's wrong?"

"Everything," Clare's muffled voice said from behind her pillow.

"Oh, Clare. It can't be that bad."

"Well, it is."

Taking a deep breath, her mother continued, "Sometimes things look really dark—sometimes so dark that we don't even believe that light can exist. But if we ask God, He will ignite a spark within us. And that spark will grow to a flame."

"I don't feel any spark, Mom. I don't even see the point anymore. Every time I try... every time I think it's going good... it's ruined. Everything is ruined. Everyone hates me! I'm not going back there! I have *no one!*"

"Oh, honey, you have me and your dad and James. And you have Jesus, who is with you always."

"What's that even supposed to mean?!"

"Take a deep breath and say a prayer. There's more to life than high school. You'll see. I'll call the school and tell them you left because you weren't feeling well. I'll check back on you in a bit, okay?"

Clare sobbed an incoherent response into her pillow, and her mom closed the door.

Thoughts swirled in Clare's mind.

Thoughts she would never admit to her mom or to anyone.

Thoughts too dark to say out loud. But they swirled nonetheless.

The self-loathing that came with such a public humiliation left her crawling in her own skin.

Who did she hate worse? Herself for making the stupid mistake—embarrassing herself in front of the most socially influential people in school—twice? Or Nikki for being the unfeeling vulture that she was?

Either way...what did it matter? She couldn't change who she was. She already tried that. She thought she could mold herself to the world's standards. She thought if she just wore the right thing or said the right thing...that she could just be...better!

What was the point? What was the point of any of it anymore? She considered what it would be like at school now...with no one at her side. She pictured herself with no one to sit next to in class, no one to talk with at lunch.

She couldn't bear it.

She imagined what it would be like to cease to exist—how Ethan had been here one day and gone the next.

Poof.

Like a hot breath on a cold day, she wondered what it would be like to disappear into an icy wind.

The seeming insignificance of her life weighed down on her as she lowered her head to her pillow and closed her eyes.

"For I know well the plans I have in mind for you—oracle of the LORD—plans for your welfare and not for woe, so as to give you a future of hope."
Jeremiah 29:11

5
Tuesday

BEEP BEEP BEEP...........BEEP BEEP BEEP...........

Clare reached over and smacked her alarm clock with disgust, not bothering to even sit up. She pulled the blanket over her head to dim the glaring morning sun.

Knock, knock, knock. "Clare, it's time to get up," her mom called from the other side of the bedroom door.

"I'm not going," Clare replied.

"Staying in bed is not going to fix whatever it is that's going on." Her mother pushed open the door and stuck her head in.

"Well, it won't hurt to try."

"Clare...if you are ready to talk to me, I'm ready to listen..."

"I don't wanna talk, Mom. I just want to be left alone."

"Okay. I'll call you in. Just this once. But tomorrow, you're going back to school." Her mother closed the door behind her as she left.

✝

A few hours later, her mother again appeared at the door, carrying a plate of scrambled eggs and toast with a side of Twix candy bar. "Eat something," she insisted, setting the plate on the bedside table. Mom knew the way to her heart.

Clare saw the candy bar and brightened.

Her mother sat down on the edge of the bed next to her. She brushed the hair back from Clare's lowered face. "If you don't want to talk to me, that's okay, but please talk to someone. Maybe try giving Caitlin a call. You two have been friends since preschool. One fight can't

63

keep you apart forever."

"She won't talk to me. Not after what happened. I don't think she'll ever be able to forgive me."

"Have you ever asked for forgiveness?"

"Well...no...not exactly."

"Sometimes, all it takes to heal a relationship is to admit that what you did or said was wrong. And that you wish you hadn't done it. Just say you're sorry, Clare. I know it feels hard to do, but it's worth it. I have to go help your brother, but I'll be up to check on you later, okay. I love you. It's going to be all right."

"Thanks, Mom."

Her mother stood, walked to the doorway, and turned back towards Clare. "Oh, and tomorrow morning I'm going to call Coach Rhonda to see if she will take you back on the team. Get back to doing the things you love, Clare. It will help." She blew Clare a kiss before turning to leave.

✝

Clare spent the day in bed, turning over all the recent events in her mind. *Why did I have to find those stupid glasses? Everything would have been fine if I had never picked them up that night. Who cares if they got thrown in the trash? That's where they belong.*

She pictured Nikki's face after she had done it, tossing them into the bin. Pure wicked satisfaction. Clare shook her head, disgusted with herself. *Why didn't I say anything or stand up for myself? If only I could have just said something to Nikki—held my own. A witty comeback. Anything would have been better than running off, blubbering like an infant. In front of everybody!* Nikki... She envisioned Nikki's venomous green eyes. *She's not even a nice person. Caitlin would never have done something like that.*

Maybe her mom was right; maybe she should just say sorry. *But I'm not the only one who did something wrong! She better say she's sorry too!* She recalled her mother, on a previous occasion, telling her to "pack away her pride" when she said something like that. "You worry about you," her mother would say, "and leave them to correct their own wrongdoing." *Ugh. That's the hard part. It's always so much easier to see what other people are doing wrong than to see it in yourself.*

She reached for her phone, pulling up her last text to Caitlin. "I HATE YOU!" in bold in that tiny speech bubble.

Guilt settled in her chest. She should say something...maybe she could say something that could fix it...

No.

She swiped left, and the conversation was forever deleted from her phone.

There. Now she wouldn't have to be reminded of that horrible day ever again.

Tap, tap, tap. A tiny hand reached around the cracked open door, and a face appeared. "Clare?" a small voice chimed. James stood in the doorway holding a bag of cheese puffs.

"Come here." Clare waved her little brother into the room. Then she helped him up onto the bed next to her and tucked him in. James reached into the large crunchy bag and pulled out an electric orange snack, offering it to his sister.

Clare smiled and popped the treat into her mouth. They sat for a bit, munching contentedly before James asked, "Why are you home?"

"Oh, buddy..." Clare didn't know how to answer—so she didn't.

"Are you sad?" he asked, gazing up at her with his big blue eyes.

Clare sighed and took his hand in hers. "Yes. I think I am."

"Sometimes I'm sad too," he answered.

"Why are you sad, buddy?" Clare asked sincerely.

"I'm sad...cus I don't remember Ethan."

"Awwww...." Clare hugged James close. "You were so little when he...died. I'm sorry. What if I tell you a story? It can help you understand who he was."

James nodded and leaned into his sister, closing his eyes.

"A couple of summers ago, we were at Camp Arrowhead—well, actually, I was at camp, and Ethan was there as a counselor. He loved camp. He said being there as a leader was the best time of his life. He loved helping the youngest ones. The first-year campers were always nervous. Many of them had never spent a week away from their families before. They would get homesick, but Ethan always had a joke and a smile for them. Anyway, one night a bad storm rolled in. A couple first years had taken out a canoe. They were out on the lake when the heavy downpour came. We all rushed to our cabins, soaking wet. I remember the sand on my feet when I climbed up into my bunk and looked out the window. They were blowing the siren to warn everybody that the storm was on its way, but it was too late. It was already on us. Then all the counselors started shouting. "Hey! Someone's still out there!" I saw the canoe overturn, and then Ethan burst out from the counselor's cabin. He didn't even look back. He ran down the winding, dirt path to the docks and dove right in. The water was coming down so hard that the splashes coming off the water made it difficult for him to breathe. One of the girls was clinging to the red canoe, but I couldn't even see the other one when Ethan dove in. But he must have because he swam right to her. They both surfaced, and some of the other older kids ran down to meet them. They helped pull her to shore. He started CPR while others grabbed another boat to help the other girl that was still out there. He got the girl breathing again. He saved her life. When he carried her up to the nurse's station, everyone was cheering like crazy from their cabins. I remember thinking, 'that's my brother.'" Clare wiped a tear from her eye.

"He was a superhero?" James asked.

Clare laughed. "Yeah, buddy, he kind of was," Clare answered, holding her little brother tighter than she ever had before.

"Finally, draw your strength from the Lord and from his mighty power. Put on the armor of God so that you may be able to stand firm against the tactics of the devil. For our struggle is not with flesh and blood but with the principalities, with the powers, with the world rulers of this present darkness, with the evil spirits in the heavens."
Ephesians 6:10-12

6
Wednesday

Clare sluggishly readied herself for the day, resisting the passing minutes with every ounce of her will. She stared up at herself in the mirror as she brushed her teeth. As she did, she muttered under her breath, "You idiot. Look at the mess you've made." *Maybe I could skip class, and Mom wouldn't notice...but where would I even go? I have no one. If I disappeared, I doubt anyone would even care...probably wouldn't even notice.* 'You have me and your dad and James,' Clare replayed her mother's words in her head.

"Yeah, but not Ethan," she answered to herself aloud.

If Ethan were here, he would tell her something that would make things feel right again. He would say something clever like, "Clare, never take to heart the opinions of people you don't respect." He actually did say that to her once. Some girls had pushed her down on the playground and called her ugly in second grade. She had come home crying with a skinned knee and a bruised ego. At the time, she didn't really understand what he had meant by it. But now, seven years later, the words held deep meaning for her.

Oh, Ethan. I wish you were here. Just come back and tell me it's going to be all right.

She wiped the toothpaste from the corners of her mouth and joined her father in the kitchen. Either he was running really late for work, or he had stayed home later that morning on purpose to get the chance to talk with her. She wasn't sure which.

72

He shuffled back and forth between the refrigerator and kitchen island, tossing things into his igloo cooler, speaking to Clare without direct eye contact. "I know things have been difficult, Clare," he said between quick sips of his coffee. "Just remember, there is life beyond high school. And your mom said Coach Rhonda is letting you back on the team! So, that's great news!"

At this, Clare rolled her eyes.

She wasn't really sure why she reacted this way. She had always loved softball. But somehow, the idea of being on a team right now—more people's expectations of her, the crowd's eyes on her—felt so unnerving.

"Dad, I don't know if now is a good time—to be back on the team and everything."

"Nonsense. Now is the perfect time," he replied casually.

"Oh, did you tell her the great news?" Clare's mom intercepted the conversation as she moved through the room with an overflowing laundry basket on her hip.

"Yeah, and she doesn't exactly seem thrilled," he responded while tossing Clare a sideways glance.

"Dad, I can't just go on with everything as if nothing has changed. The girls probably don't even want me back on the team."

Her mom rejoined them in the kitchen, dropping a weighty bag of softball supplies down in front of Clare. "Honey, the girls will get over it. But Coach did say that this is your last chance. If you skip any more practices, you'll be off the team for good. So, don't forget, practice is tonight from five-thirty to seven-thirty. I won't be home this afternoon to remind you because James has swim class, but I'll see you when you get home for dinner. I'm making lasagna—you're favorite." She kissed Clare on the forehead and shuffled back out of the room.

"I gotta go, Boo, but I'll see you tonight at dinner. Don't forget, God doesn't give you more

74

than you can handle. You got this." Her dad shut the house door.

"Sure. I've got this," Clare ranted to herself as she grabbed a Pop-Tart and her backpack and headed out into the painfully bright, cheery day. "They literally have no idea. What do they know about my life and what it feels like to be a teenage girl whose friends have abandoned her?"

☦

With the unusually warm October weather, the students were gathered in social circles on the school's front steps as Clare pulled up on her bike.

She spotted Elise and Nikki, positioned unavoidably centerstage on the first landing.

They spotted her as well.

They glared at her and then looked at each other, throwing their heads back in laughter. It was all so ugly.

After having sincerely considered going straight back home to her bedroom to bury her face in her pillow, Clare accepted the eventuality that she must go and pushed past the girls, avoiding eye contact. Their snickering only increased. Self-loathing thoughts crept into Clare's mind as she climbed the last steps and pulled open the sticky, fingerprinted doors.

Once inside, she made her way to her locker, quickly gathered her books, and slammed the door shut.

"Holy crap! Are you trying to give me a heart attack?!" Clare exclaimed.

Noah had been standing on the other side of the door. "Sorry, I didn't mean to scare you. I just wanted to give these back. You should really be more careful with them, ya know." He handed Clare the now slightly scratched aviator sunglasses.

"Oh, yeah. Umm, thanks," she replied, taking them gingerly from him and sliding them on top of her head like a headband. He gave her a knowing look and turned away.

She pivoted back towards her locker, pausing to digest what had happened. *What was that look? Does he know?*

She glanced back in his direction, but he had already gone into the classroom at the end of the hall. *He must have had the glasses since Monday when Nikki chucked them into the bin. Why would he have taken them out of the garbage? And why would he bother returning them to me? If he saw what I saw...he wouldn't just give them back like that, would he?* Clare puzzled through, trying to put herself in Noah's place.

Thoughts of what Noah might or might not know filled her mind the following few class periods. By lunch, she couldn't even remember what the English topic had been, nor History or Science. At least for the time being, she wasn't preoccupied with what to do about Nikki. That was until she was standing at the lunchroom door holding a tray, and there wasn't a friendly face in the room to join. *This is so humiliating. What kind of loser has to eat alone?*

The situation felt all too familiar to her as she recalled her terrifying dream from a few nights ago.

Off to the left, she spotted an empty table. She walked over, clunked the plastic tray down, and resigned to her new social low. She picked at her cold pizza for the next twenty minutes and shoved some fluffy pink stuff around with her spoon, impatiently waiting for the bell to ring. Then she heard a soft voice behind her say, "Can I sit here?" It was Caitlin.

Startled, Clare responded, "Oh, hi. Yes, sure."

Caitlin sat down next to her, fidgeting an apple from hand to hand. She looked over at Clare with sincerity in her eyes. "I heard about what happened in the hall the other day with Nikki. And then you didn't come back to school. I guess I was just wondering if you are okay...?"

Surprised by the kindness, Clare felt like bursting into tears. Her throat tightened, and before she even knew what to say, the words spilled out. "Caitlin, I'm so sorry. It was all my fault. I knew I shouldn't have gone off to party with Elise and Colton the night of your birthday. And I never should have expected you to lie for me. When I said 'I hate you'...I didn't mean it. I was just so mad that my mom found out. Can you ever forgive me?"

A single tear fell from Caitlin's eye as she nodded 'yes.' "Just please don't ever ask me to cover for you again, Clare," Caitlin replied.

"I won't. I promise." Clare took Caitlin's hand.

"Cait, if I tell you something, do you swear you won't have me committed to an asylum?"

Caitlin tilted her head as she studied Clare and held up her pinky finger. And just like when they were little girls, Clare looped her pinky around Caitlin's and shook twice. "Promise."

Clare inhaled deeply and began, "I think I'm losing my mind. Will you please look through these and tell me what you see?" She took the glasses off her head and slid them over to Caitlin, who looked suspiciously from the glasses to Clare and back again before picking them up and putting them on her face. Without a change in expression, she took them off and set them in front of Clare.

"Well?!" Clare asked, leaning forward, both hands on the table.

"Well, I see a crowded lunchroom."

"And?!"

"And some extremely bright angelic beings with some demons prowling about in the corners."

Clare's eyes just about bugged out of her head.

She jumped up from her seat impulsively before realizing she might cause a scene and quickly sat back down. "Caitlin! You see them too?!" Clare's intensity reached fever pitch. "How are you not freaking out right now?!"

"Ummm...ha...I guess...well, I guess I've always known they were there...so...it didn't come as a surprise? I have to admit, though, I had no idea they would be so beautiful."

"Beautiful?! They're disgusting!"

"Oh, you mean the demons? Yeah, I guess they are pretty gross, but I could barely even see them through the shining brightness of the angels. Wow. You see what you're looking for, I guess."

Clare scrunched her eyebrows in thought and put the glasses back on. Caitlin was right. The angels far outnumbered the demons. There must have been at least one for every student in the room. "They're angels? And demons? Are you sure?"

"Don't know what else they would be? I mean, we're surrounded by the spiritual world. We're in battle, ya know."

"C'mon, Cait. Are you going to tell me that vampires and werewolves are real too? Because I was actually a lot more comfortable when I thought I was going nuts. You mean to tell me these things have always been around?"

Just then, the bell rang. Everyone rose from their seats and began shuffling toward their destinations.

Caitlin leaned over and whispered to Clare, "Meet me in the library tomorrow for third-period study hall. I want to show you something."

Clare nodded and squeezed Caitlin in a one-armed hug. "Thank you."

Caitlin smiled and headed to class.

There was a new lightness to Clare's step. It was like some invisible weight had lifted off her shoulders. She wasn't going crazy. And she wasn't alone.

✝

The afternoon passed quickly, and Clare avoided any trouble with Nikki and Elise by skipping out of school just five minutes early.

Back at home, she made herself a snack and flipped on the TV. James' annoying preschool sing-alongs usually dominated the family viewing, but with everyone gone, she could watch whatever she wanted. She scrolled through Netflix, searching for something that didn't suck. She finally chose a random reality show about people who get married before even setting eyes on each other. The mindless show was a welcome distraction.

Time slipped by. At 5:00, Clare's phone alarm went off. "GO TO PRACTICE!" blinked on and off on her screen. "Crap, I almost forgot," she said aloud as she jumped off the couch and threw on her softball gear, swung her backpack over her shoulder, and headed back out the door. If she was even five minutes late, Coach would make her do twenty-five push-ups in front of the whole team.

She made it to the field in time, sweating. The afternoon sun was already hanging low in the sky. The sound of balls thumping into gloves and cracking off bats was comforting to Clare in a way. Some of the girls greeted Clare with a smile but most responded to Clare's return to the team with a glare. They didn't appreciate a teammate who only followed through when she felt like it. And they probably didn't appreciate that Coach Rhonda kept giving Clare more chances.

As Clare hustled through the team drills, Coach made her way over.

"Thomson. Good to see you back."

"Good to be back, Coach," Clare replied.

"This is your last shot, kiddo."

Clare hated being called pet names like kiddo, but she held back her attitude and nodded respectfully in response.

84

"All right, girls!" Coach called out as she clapped her hands together a few times. "Split into teams! Scrimmage! Jackson, Thiel, Schmitt, and Hawly get into the outfield. Thomson, you're up to bat first! Hustle!" *Clap, clap, clap.*

Clare ran to the dugout and grabbed her bat while smacking her batting helmet onto her head. She looked down at the fat end of the bat squeezed between her feet as she strapped the Velcro on her gloves. She heard some voices approaching. It was Elise and Finn. "Hey, Clare! Back on the team, huh?" Elise yelled while leaning up against the chain-link fence.

"I said hustle, Thomson! Get it together!" Coach's voice rang out. The pitcher was already in position and clearly impatient.

Without responding to Elise, Clare stepped up to the plate. The first pitch came in fast and to the inside. Clare swung hard and missed. "Strike one!" Coach called out. The second pitch was high. "Ball! Good eye, Thomson!"

Third pitch. Right in the zone. Clare swung. *Whack!* "Run! Run! Run!" the girls called out. Clare's speed was second to none on the team. She ran through first base before the outfielder could throw it in.

"Nice work, kid!" Coach slapped hands with Clare at first base.

"Thanks," Clare said sincerely. She was smiling. It felt good. Like maybe things could go back to normal.

"Not too bad, Clare!" Elise shouted from the bleachers.

Well, that's unexpected. Clare figured Elise and Finn were only at the field looking for a new place to make out. Her words of encouragement after everything that had happened came as quite a surprise.

After stealing the next two bases and then being hit in for a run, the girls switched to playing defense. Clare was sent to cover left field. By this time, the sun was angled just right to poke her directly in the eye if she were to tilt her head up. *I'll never be able to catch a pop fly like this.* Clare quickly ran to the dugout, grabbed her sunglasses, and jogged back to position. She looked around, relieved to find the only thing unusual in her view was that Elise and Finn weren't hanging on each other.

A petite blond girl everyone called 'Smalls' took the base.

She was a player the other teams consistently underestimated. At the first pitch, she took a wild swing at a high ball that was clearly out of her batting zone; she connected, sending it flying directly at Clare. "I got it! I got it!" Clare shouted to her hovering teammates.

She was jogging backward, not taking her eye off the ball. She threw her left hand up while giving a little jump and *whap*; she caught it.

87

"Yes!" Clare hollered as she whipped the ball back to the pitcher.

Maybe her mom was right. She just needed to get back to what she loved, and it would all be okay. Clare then glanced back up towards the new batter, swinging her practice swings while taking the plate. She could see Elise and Finn in her periphery.

Wait, what was that?

Two shadowy forms blew past her on both sides. They raced towards Elise.

Without thinking, Clare shouted out, "NO! Get away from her!" She took off running towards the bleachers while swinging her arms. "Stop it! Stop it!" she shouted.

At this, both of the demons swung around in a sweeping loop. They rounded Elise—who was now looking embarrassed and confused—and turned, glaring directly at Clare. They appeared to be growling and hissing at her. Clare quickly realized her mistake.

The demons could smell Elise's temptation, and now they could taste Clare's fear. Exploiting weakness was their only motivation.

What was I thinking?! If they didn't know I could see them before, they certainly know it now! She immediately started backing away, completely unaware of the laughter and comments that were going on around her.

The demons rushed at her.

Clare fell backward but swiftly jumped to her feet.

She took off at a dead run, pushing past the pitcher, knocking her off balance.

Clare flew across the outfield.

The demons surrounded her, but she kept running.

She slipped through the gap in the chain-link fence and hit the sidewalk.

She knew where she had to go.

Sweating and waving her arms hysterically, she scrambled up the steps of St. Anne's. "Please be unlocked! Please be unlocked!" she yelled as she yanked open the doors. "Yes! Thank you, Jesus!" She wasn't swearing. She truly meant it.

She collapsed onto her knees, panting.

The glasses fell off her face, and she burst into tears. The cold marble floors, smooth against her hands, felt as if they were the only thing keeping her from melting into hell itself at that moment. She lay there on the floor, sobbing, for what was surely hours.

It was dark now. The usually vivid stained glass windows were now murky and lifeless.

A prance of claws clicked near the far East entrance, echoing off the plastered walls. "Hello?" a deep, husky voice penetrated the silence.

Clare sat up, sniffed forcefully, and answered, "Yes, Father, it's just me."

"Clare? Is that you, Clare Thomson?" Father Mike and Charlie shuffled into the nave, the dog leading towards where Clare was still sitting on the floor.

"Clare. It's almost 9:00. I was just going to lock up. What are you doing here?"

"Oh, Father. You wouldn't believe me if I told you."

"Has someone hurt you? Your voice is shaking."

"Will you call my mom for me? I don't have my phone."

"Of course, I will," Father Mike said as he moved towards the sacristy, Charlie at his side. "Why don't you come sit up here? I'll be back shortly." He gestured towards the first pew with his cane. Clare sluggishly moved to where he had pointed and listened as she heard him speaking on the phone from the other room.

He returned and sat down next to her, the large gray dog getting comfortable at his feet.

"Your mom is on her way. She told me she's been worried about you. She said you never came home after softball and that your coach had called to tell her that you ran off the field mid-practice."

He paused, leaving her to fill in the blanks.

"Father, last Sunday in your homily...you said something about Satan falling from heaven...and demons prowling about the earth...seeking the ruin of souls...or something like that..."

"Yes?"

"Well...I think...well... I'm pretty sure... I've been attacked...by demons."

"Why do you think you are being attacked?"

"...I think it's because I yelled at them."

"You yelled at them?" Father asked. Even though he was wearing his typical dark sunglasses, she could tell he was raising one eyebrow.

"Yes. I yelled at them to get away from my friends."

"How did you know they were there...with your friends?"

Clare paused, stirring in her seat.

Father took a deep breath and began, "Clare,

we are all in a spiritual battle. It sounds as if you are worried about your friends—that you might fear that they are going down the wrong path."

"Father...does evil exist? I mean, is it real?"

"Well, the simple answer is yes. Let me try to explain. Evil isn't exactly a thing itself. It is a lack of a good that should be present in a thing. So, evil is actually an absence. But yes, evil, like good, is an objective reality."

"So, demons...are they real then as well? Like, are they living all around us?"

"Some people will tell you that the devil is merely a symbol of evil. But demons are personal spiritual beings—fallen angels—and the devil is one of them. You mentioned that I said that Satan fell from the heavens down to earth."

Clare nodded.

"You see, when God created angels, He subjected them to a test—a *divine* test. They were to be permitted to see God at His very essence. This is called the Beatific Vision. But before He allowed this, He tested their faithfulness. Demons were not created evil, but when they refused to worship Jesus, who was in the form of a human, some rebelled. Being the purely intellectual creatures that they are, the fallen angels considered themselves above humans. In Job 4:18, we read, 'In His angels, He found wickedness.' They were transformed into demons when they rebelled and were cast out of heaven. So, just like the Saint Michael prayer says, evil creatures really are prowling about the world seeking the ruin of souls."

"But Father, if these creatures are real and want to...ruin our souls, what can we even do about it? I mean, how can we fight back against something we can't even...see?"

"Trust me. We don't need to be able to see to fight back," he began, smiling. "The battle is spiritual, not physical, so we need to fight spiritually—through prayer, penance, and even fasting. All of these things keep evil at bay. St. Therese of Lisieux tells us that 'a soul in the state of grace has nothing to fear from demons, who are cowards capable of running away from the look of a child.' Speaking the name of Jesus and believing in His power is enough to frighten the most determined demon away. They can't stand even the sound of His holy name."

"How do you know all this, Father? And how do you know it's true?"

"Jesus, Himself, was tempted by the devil. After Jesus had been baptized, He went into the desert to fast for forty days and forty nights. During this time, Satan appeared to Jesus and tried to tempt him three times. You can read about it in your Bible when you get home, in Matthew 4:1-11. I've also read extensively the writings of the Church Fathers who warn us of such evil and how to prepare for it. I happen to know a fellow priest who is an exorcist. His stories alone are sufficient to convince the most hardened skeptic that evil spirits are truly present here on earth."

"What's an exorcist?" Clare inquired.

"An exorcist is a priest who frees people possessed by a demon. Possessed, as in a demon has taken over a person's body. Did you know that every Catholic diocese in America has at least one exorcist?"

"What?! They can take over my body?!" Clare suddenly shrieked.

Startled, Father Mike responded, "It's nothing to be afraid of, dear! You need to *allow* a demon in for that to happen. If you are in the state of grace, you have nothing to fear, like I said. Being in the state of grace means that you are without the stain of sin on your soul. You see, sin draws us away from God. Sin is, as you know, any act that violates the law written on the heart of every person, God's law. Sin draws us away from God. God never leaves us, but we can turn away from Him through our choices. He gave us free will. He only wants us to love Him, and love cannot be forced. It must be freely given. That's why God allows sin and evil to work in the world. He wants us to choose

Him and His will for our lives over our own selfish desires for pleasure and comfort. If you steer clear of sin, you have nothing to fear from demons."

"Why doesn't God just annihilate all the demons?" Clare asked.

"God, in his great love, has pledged not to destroy any intelligent being He created. Demons, by their very existence, are a manifestation of God's justice. They are terrifying proof of the divine order. In a certain sense, even the demons enrich the perfect order of God's creation. Beauty cannot be destroyed by ugliness; rather, ugliness, or evil, makes us see beauty all the more by contrast.[1] It's like the welcome warmth of spring after an especially harsh winter. Without experiencing the darkness and bitter cold, we wouldn't be able to properly appreciate the heat and warmth of the sun.

"I wish God had never created the angels." Clare stared down at her hands. "Then they never would have been able to rebel and become demons."

"I can understand that sentiment. But God makes no mistakes. He loves all of His creations. But Clare, once you have seen darkness, the light appears even brighter, does it not?"

"How do you mean?"

"Oh, Clare! I've been worried sick!" Clare's mother exclaimed, bursting into the sanctuary. "Father Mike, thank you so much for calling. C'mon, Clare, let me get you home."

Clare got up and glanced back at Father Mike. "Thank you," she said. "Mom, we need to go pick up my bike."

"Okay, honey. That's no problem," her mom said as she took Clare's hand.

Clare put on her sunglasses as her mom gently tugged her into the doorway. She glanced back just before the heavy wooden doors slammed shut behind her. Through the gap, she saw that the entire church was filled with the most glorious light. And painted on the wall in Latin was 'INDUITE VOS ARMATURUM DEI UT POSSITIS STARE ADVERSUS INSIDIAS DIABOLI.'

"For, although we are in the flesh, we do not battle according to the flesh, for the weapons of our battle are not of flesh but are enormously powerful, capable of destroying fortresses."
2 Corinthians 10:3-4

7
Thursday

Clare's bloodshot eyes stung as she woke the following day.

She had tossed and turned, waking several times during the night with a start, eventually resigning herself to sleeping with the lights on. She couldn't shake the memories of the previous evening and the dark presence she now sensed, haunting her.

Although she kept the glasses close by, she never dared put them on to see what may be with her—there in her bedroom—there in her own home.

"Great," she said as she threw off her blankets, "now I'm not only tormented by Nikki, but by demons too."

She dragged herself out of bed and dressed quickly. And without the attention to detail that she typically gave her make-up routine, she left the house and headed for school.

Everything she did now felt rushed, hurried, frantic. Although Father Mike had told her that the demons only inhabit those that have surrendered to them, she was still on edge. The only solace was knowing that her friendship with Caitlin had been restored. She looked forward to study hall, where they could talk.

The bell rang through the school halls, indicating that third period was about to begin. Clare weaved through the bustling students, anxious to join Caitlin in the library.

Jefferson High was one of the oldest buildings in town, and its library held an extensive collection of first editions. Anything a person needed to know could be learned there.

"Where do you think you're going?" Nikki's voice was unmistakable.

Clare flinched and paused as Nikki moved assertively between her and the library doors. "Ya know, for a minute, I thought you had it in ya—to be one of us. But here you are again, slummin' it with the losers." Nikki glanced from Clare to Caitlin, who could be seen through the library doors waving at Clare. Nikki smiled smugly.

"Yeah...I don't know, Nikki. Lately, I'm beginning to wonder who the real losers are," Clare responded without making eye contact.

"What did you just say?" Nikki stepped closer to Clare, posturing her shoulders.

"Nothing, Nikki. Forget it," Clare said as she attempted to move past Nikki. Nikki only side-stepped and positioned herself, again, directly in front of Clare.

"You better watch yourself, Clare Bear. I think you've started to forget who I *am* and who you are *not*."

Clare quickly stepped around Nikki and through the large double doors.

Caitlin was standing at a long wooden table, waving at Clare to join her. There was an impressive stack of books in front of her. "What was that about?" Caitlin asked, gesturing with her chin towards the hallway.

"It was nothing," Clare replied.

"Didn't look like nothing."

"I never should have tried to be in with them in the first place. It was easier before. Soooo, before we get to whatever you have going on here—" Clare waved her hands in circles over the towering stack of books on the table, "—there's something I have to tell you." She plunked down in the chair across from Caitlin.

"Okay," Caitlin responded, wide-eyed with anticipation.

"Yesterday, I was at softball practice, and I yelled...at the demons."

"What?! I imagine that didn't go over well." Caitlin grimaced.

"Yeah. No, it didn't. They chased me. I ran all the way to St. Anne's. Somehow I knew they wouldn't be able to follow me in. It was horrible. I'd never been so scared in my life."

"Clare, why didn't you call out to your guardian angel for help?"

"What? I don't know. Wait, what are you talking about?"

"Your guardian angel. Ya know, 'angel of God, my guardian dear, to whom God's love commits me here. Ever this night, be at my side, to light and guard, to rule and guide. Amen.' The prayer they taught us when we were kids."

"Cait, I stopped saying that years ago, back when my mom stopped tucking me in at night. I thought that was just something parents told kids to say to make them feel better or something."

"Actually, I've been reading up on it, and that prayer has been said for centuries. Saint Basil tells us that 'beside each believer stands an angel as protector, and shepherd, leading him to life.' Do you know why the angels are so bright that they are hard to look at? It's because they gaze on the face of God, who is light itself. Here, let me show you." Caitlin pulled a thick book titled 'Holy Bible' off the stack and opened it up for Clare to see. "See," she continued, "here in Matthew 18:10, it says, 'angels in heaven always look upon the face of my heavenly Father.' Angels actually get to be with God in heaven! They have His blessing and power to help us if it is His will! Give me the glasses, quick!"

Clare reached over and handed the aviators to Caitlin and sat down expectantly.

"Clare! You have two!" Caitlin said, just a little too loud for the librarian, who glared at the girls from her desk.

"Two what?' Clare responded.

"Two guardian angels!" Caitlin exclaimed. "I read that most people have one, but God grants some people two and even sometimes three angels to protect them. Clare! You are so lucky! Here! Put them on, look around and tell me how many I have!"

"Ummm, well, I see one over there about fifteen feet behind you near the magazine rack. I can't see his face, but he seems really intent on you. I think that one is yours. Yours? Is that okay to say? I mean, it's not like they belong to us...like a dog or something, right? I'm new to this, Cait. Tell me what's going on here exactly."

"Oh, man. I was really hoping I would have three." Caitlin's shoulders slumped, and her lips pursed.

"Well, maybe that one over there hovering over the librarian's left shoulder is actually yours, and he just likes the smell of her perfume or something?" Clare smirked. She shrugged, and Caitlin laughed and reached over to the books once more.

Caitlin pulled another book off the stack and scooted over next to Clare, opening up a title called Angels (and Demons) What Do We Really Know About Them by Peter Kreeft. "Okay. So I've been reading all night. Look here, on page 53, it says,

'Angels were created before the dawn of time. They sang at the creation of the world. Some rebelled against God, became demons or devils (evil spirits), and set up hell's lowerarchy against heaven's hierarchy. One of them was the snake in the grass that tempted us to give up paradise. Angels were instrumental at every major stage of God's plan to get us back on the road to paradise. They surrounded the life of Abraham, the first of God's "chosen people." They announced to Sarah, his hundred-year-old, laughing wife, that she would have a miracle baby. They stopped him from making a human sacrifice of Isaac. They saved Abraham and his nephew Lot from the foretaste of hell that destroyed Sodom and Gomorrah. They came to

Jacob in the desert on a ladder, back and forth like eighteen-wheelers on that busy highway to heaven. One picked up the prophet Habakkuk by the hair and whisked him seven hundred miles away. Angels came to old women and old men, to the blind and the poor, to shepherds and fleeing criminals, but not to kings or politicians. One came to a teenaged Jewish girl as an ambassador of her Creator and meekly asked her permission in his name to use her womb as his door into our world. And because she said Yes to his angel, we have Christmas, and Easter, and the hope of heaven.' [2]

"Clare! We were given a gift!" Caitlin exclaimed, her face beaming. "We can see divine history! One of these angels could have been the one who declared to Mary that she would bear the son of God! This is amazing!"

"I'm sure you're right. I mean, I know you're right. It *is* amazing. I love learning about the angels, Cait, but I am a *little* more interested in learning how to defeat these demons right now.

You do remember me telling you I was attacked last night, don't you? And now that they know I can see them, I've been feeling more haunted than ever."

"Oh right, yeah. Okay. Here, look at this." Caitlin opened yet another book to share with Clare. "Here, I found this epic book called Interview with an Exorcist by Father Jose Antonio Fortea. On page 25, he answers the question 'Should we be afraid of the devil?' by saying, 'The devil strives to do all the evil that he can, especially by tempting us to turn away from God through sin. If he could do more evil, he would. If a person prays the Rosary daily and asks God to protect him from all snares from the Evil One, he has nothing to fear. The power of God is infinite; that of the devil is not.' " [3]

"And here it says, 'St. Paul tells us, INDUITE VOS ARMATURUM DEI UT POSSITIS STARE ADVERSUS INSIDIAS DIABOLI,' (Ephesians 6:11)."

"That's what it says in our church! Painted on the walls above the arches in the nave! What does it mean?" Clare interjected.

"It says here below in italics that it's Latin for 'put on the whole armor of God that you may be able to stand against the wiles of the devil.' "

"I can't believe that's been right in front of me all this time, and I never understood." Clare shook her head.

Caitlin began again, "It also says here, 'We know that no one begotten by God sins; but the one begotten by God he protects, and the evil one cannot touch him. (1 John 5:18). And Jesus Himself assures us: Behold, I have given you the power 'to tread upon serpents' and scorpions and upon the full force of the enemy and nothing will harm you. (Luke 10:19) Sin not and trust in the Lord, for Faith in God casts out all fear.'

"See, Clare, you have nothing to fear."

"No, Cait," Clare replied. "It says anyone that *does not sin* has nothing to fear. But what about me? I'm just a normal girl. I'm no saint!"

"All of the saints were just normal people, Clare—normal people who surrendered their lives to Christ with trust and love. We're all called to be saints. A saint is just someone who is in heaven. That's what we're all called to."

"Me? A saint? Ha...you said faith in God casts out all fear...Caitlin, if I believe in God, then why am I still afraid?"

"I don't know. Maybe...maybe you believe in God...but you don't *know* Him yet."

"Do you know Him, Cait?"

"I think so. I mean, I know I have a lot to learn, but I know that I can't do anything without Him. He's the reason I am breathing right now. And He gives meaning to my suffering. My identity is in Him, not social media or in my popularity at school. I'm a daughter of the King. That stuff with Nikki—in the halls every day—I know Christ suffered far more. When it gets hard, I lay my pain at the feet of His cross. The Bible, in Matthew 5:10-12, tells us, 'Blessed are they who are persecuted for the sake of righteousness, for theirs is the kingdom of heaven. Blessed are you when they insult you and persecute you and utter every kind of evil against you [falsely] because of me. Rejoice and be glad, for your reward will be great in heaven. Thus they persecuted the prophets who were before you.' "

"Caitlin, when did you get so...Christian?"

"I've been going to classes on Wednesdays. I'm getting confirmed this Easter, Clare."

"Wow. So, you're all in now, huh?"

"Yeah. I'm all in now."

"Okay...okay. All right. Hey, all right," Clare replied, smiling as she patted Caitlin on the back.

"Hey!" Caitlin stood up quickly. "There was one more book I wanted to show you, but I couldn't find it on the shelf. Let's ask the librarian to check if it's here somewhere I didn't think to look." Caitlin stood up quickly.

The girls quietly crossed the now crowded room to the large oval desk.

"Excuse me," Caitlin said softly.

"Yes? How can I help you?" the librarian replied, peering over the tops of her reading glasses.

"Hi. I haven't been able to find a book titled Imagine Heaven by John Burke. Can you tell me whether it's here?"

"Of course. Just one moment...yes, we have a copy, but it looks like it's checked out right now. Would you like me to put you on the waitlist?"

"I don't think that will be necessary, ma'am," Noah said as he approached the girls. "I have a copy at home. I'll lend it to you. It's no problem." He looked at Clare as he spoke, holding eye contact just a bit too long.

"Miss, should I put you on the list or not?" asked the librarian curtly.

"No, ma'am. Thank you anyway," Clare replied, her eyes narrowing with suspicion as she stared at Noah.

"What? Are you stalking me now?" Clare whispered harshly as the three walked back towards their table.

"Yeah, well, kinda, I think," Noah smirked.

Clare noticed an expression of amused shock pass across Caitlin's face.

"Yeah, well, I don't really need a stalker right now," Clare replied to Noah.

"I get it. Let me drop the book off to you this afternoon, and I'll explain then. You live in the white house with the porch on the corner of Section and 8th, right?"

"And you're not a stalker?!" Clare replied incredulously.

"I've seen you over there mowing the lawn on more than one occasion. Also, my sister Ava has been there before. She knew Ethan. They were classmates, and I think, friends."

"Oh...yeah, Ethan always had a pile of friends hanging around. All right. I guess I'll see you later, then?"

"You'll see me later," Noah replied, smiling as he turned to go.

"What was that about?" Caitlin asked as she prodded Clare with a smirk.

"I dunno." Clare shrugged.

"I think he likes you."

"Yeah, or he's just a creep, creepin'."

"He's never seemed the creep type to me, Clare. Always seemed more like the handsome, loyal boyfriend type actually," Caitlin replied, winking.

Clare laughed. "Okay, stop. I'm sure he was just trying to be helpful."

The bell rang.

"Well, I guess we'll find out *later*," Caitlin joked.

"I guess we will. See you at lunch!" Clare called as she gathered her things and headed for her next class.

Knock, knock, knock.

From her room, Clare heard the front door open and Noah's deep voice as he introduced himself to her father. "He's so...polite," Clare commentated to herself in a whisper, her forehead wrinkling.

"Clare! There's a boy here to see you!" Clare's father hollered up the steps.

After a quick check in the mirror, Clare shuffled down the stairs. Noah and her father both stood in the entryway, watching her intently as she made her way down to join them.

"Hey." Clare shifted her body from side to side awkwardly.

"Hey. I brought the book."

"Dinner will be ready in about twenty—oh, hi! I didn't realize we had company!" Clare's mom shouted from the kitchen.

"Well, we don't, really, Mom. Noah just stopped by to drop something off for me."

"Well, come on in for a bit! Sit down! I just made some banana bread! It's still warm!" Her mother appeared in the doorway, ushering everyone into the slightly cluttered but cozy living room.

"I can't say 'no' to banana bread," Noah replied warmly.

Clare laughed nervously. *Could this get any more awkward?!*

Noah and her dad sat down on opposite sides of the sofa while Clare chose the recliner. Seeing her dad and Noah together in her living room had her feeling like she had walked into an alternate universe. Weirdly, Noah didn't seem to mind. He actually appeared quite...comfortable.

Clare's mom returned with a steaming plate of buttered bread, the heavenly scent of vanilla and banana wafting into the room with her.

"Oh, wow. Thank you, Mrs. Thomson," Noah said, taking a thick slice. "This looks amazing."

Clare's father chatted with Noah, asking about the sports he's interested in and where he planned to attend university. Clare remained largely absent from the conversation, rocking on the paisley recliner, a bit lost in the strangeness of it all.

After a third helping of banana bread and a not-so-optional glass of milk insisted upon him by Clare's mom, Noah stood up. "Well, I better get going."

"You're welcome to stay for dinner," Clare's mom said.

"Thank you. Maybe another time. I really have to get back home. They'll be starting the Rosary soon, and I can't be late. Thank you for everything, Mrs. T. It was really nice. And nice meeting you, Mr. Thomson." He made eye contact with Clare's father and shook his hand.

"Oh, here, Clare. I almost forgot." He handed Clare a shiny, softcover book. Their eyes met.

"Thanks," is all Clare could think to say.

The door shut.

"Well, he was nice, Clare!" Clare's mom said enthusiastically.

"Yeah, he's nice," Clare replied.

"Not that I can approve of a boy—but if there was a boy that I would approve of, it would be *that* young man." Clare's father nodded.

"OOOOkay. No one has to do any approving or disapproving because he only came over to drop off a book for me. The library didn't have a copy, but he did, so that's all there is to it. The end." Clare got up. "I think I hear James on the intercom. I'll get him." She was searching for any excuse to leave that room.

She ran up the stairs, passing by James' room—there was no crying toddler after all—and closed herself in her bedroom. She plopped on the bed, opening up the book entitled *Imagine Heaven – Near-Death Experiences. God's Promises, And the Exhilarating Future That Awaits You.* Pages were dog-eared, lines were highlighted, and dozens of notes were in the margins. "Whoa, this guy didn't just read this book; he studied it," Clare mumbled.

Clare paged through to find entire paragraphs highlighted. A note in the margins read, 'read this when things get too hard to take.' It was next to a woman's description of heaven. She had died briefly and woke again to find herself technically deceased but more alive than she ever had been on Earth. She went on to illustrate a place of indescribable beauty and a feeling of intense peace.

Clare paged again to find another report of a near-death experience and yet another firsthand description of heaven. And then another. And another. The accounts differed slightly but had surprisingly consistent themes.

Can this be real?

Clare rose and went to her computer. She typed in the names of those quoted to find websites and interviews. Some of them had even written their own books testifying to their experiences.

The people. The stories. They're real.

Clare clapped the book shut and held it tightly to her chest, her heart swelling with a profound feeling she didn't at first recognize. It was a feeling of hope.

Hope wasn't something familiar to Clare. She thought back, her head foggy with memories of darker days:

It had been raining all day. Clare refused to get out of the car. She sat in her damp black dress coat, staring down at her nyloned legs. Tiny beads of water clung to the almost microscopic netting that masked her cold, blood-shot legs. Her feet crammed into the shiny black pumps her mom had purchased for her the year before to wear to her cousin's wedding. *These* shoes with *those* memories didn't feel appropriate. Dancing shoes don't belong at the burial of her beloved brother.

The drizzle continued to come down on the car windows, blurring the view of her family huddled around her brother's casket under that stupid tarp canopy. It belonged covering an eggroll vendor on the sidewalk of a farmer's market, not at a funeral, mocking her, feigning shelter when it provided no warmth or safety. The blue fabric flapped in the ever-increasing gusts. The priest stood, Bible open at the end of the casket. A pair of black-suited men held umbrellas over him, attempting to keep the rain off the large black book.

Why black? Clare pondered. *If we're supposed to believe he's at peace or be happy for him or whatever, why not white? Or vivid, joyful colors like we see at Easter celebrations?* She recalled an elderly woman who smelled of mothballs and dead roses gripping her hands together in hers while saying, "He's in a better place, dear."

If he's in a better place, then why all the morbid? How can I believe he's in a better place with everyone crying and shaking their heads in despair?!

Clare shook her head, clearing the memory from her mind like she would reset an Etch A Sketch. She opened the book again. This time a handwritten note fell out onto her lap. She picked it up and unfolded it carefully. It read,

"Clare, meet me at Calvary Cemetery. Tonight. 9 PM.

Bring Caitlin if you like.

P.S. Don't forget the glasses.

-NOAH"

✝

Clare was lying flat on her bed, staring up at the ceiling. Exhausted. Confused.

She could see the faded outlines of stars where there had once been glow in the dark decals.

What really happens when we die? Why does Noah want to meet in a cemetery?

Overwhelmed, she closed her eyes, hoping she might open them to an understanding of what all this might mean. She needed another opinion.

She whipped out her phone and typed a text to Caitlin. "...AND he invited us to meet him at Calvary Cemetery tonight at 9," she wrote. "What do you think?"

"I think you were right about him being a creep, after all!" Caitlin retorted.

"Yeah, idk though. I think it's important. He didn't seem like a freak when he was over tonight. C'mon, Cait. He invited us both."

"Yeah...idk. Are your parents even going to let you go? I thought you were on house arrest?"

"Yeah, that might be a problem...I could just sneak out."

"Or, you could try being honest with them," Caitlin suggested coolly.

"*Or*, I could try being honest with them. That is a thought..."

"All right. Let me know how that goes. I'm in if you are actually allowed to go, k. TTYL."

"Ciao, Bella," Clare typed, then clicked off her phone.

She took a deep breath, jumped up from the bed, and hustled down the stairs to the living room, where her dad was watching the news and her mom was reading a book.

"Mom, Dad—Noah invited Caitlin and me to meet up with him tonight. Now, before you say anything, I want to say how sorry I am for not always being honest with you in the past. I haven't always made the right choices, but Caitlin and I have been talking, and I realize now that I need to be more transparent with you."

The room was silent for a moment.

"Wow, Clare. I'm so pleased to hear you say these things," her mom replied.

"Where did you say you would meet him?" her father inquired, raising both eyebrows.

"...at Calvary...Cemetery," Clare responded hesitantly.

Her parents' faces flinched. "What?!" Her father's mouth hung open.

"Yeah, I was worried you would be concerned about that," Clare explained. "He doesn't mean any harm. He just wants to show us something."

"Show you what, exactly?" Clare's mother questioned.

"I don't know. But Caitlin can meet me here, and we can ride over there together. And when we get there, I will FaceTime you so you can see everything is okay. And I promise I'll be home by 10:30. I'll even text you before I ride home so you know I'm on my way. How does that sound?"

"Sounds pretty reasonable, actually..." Clare's father glanced at her mother to gauge her reaction. "Yes, all right. This is your shot to show us you are turning a new leaf, young lady."

"Yes, I understand, Dad." Clare stepped over and hugged him, awkwardly. "Thank you!"

Giddy, she ran up to her bedroom to text Caitlin the plan.

✝

Caitlin was right on time. 8:45. "Hi, Mrs. Thomson!" She cheerily greeted the family standing in the doorway.

As the two girls slid onto their bikes to leave, Clare's mother yelled, "Be careful!"

Clare waved and smiled back.

They glided down the dark streets, the smell of fall in the air. Some stray leaves fell from the trees, ground into the pavement by their racing tires.

Calvary Cemetery was just down the road from St. Anne's, and although Clare still had the demons on her mind, Caitlin's faith-filled presence was reassuring to her. They pulled up and leaned their bikes against the chain-link fence, arriving just in time to hear the church bells chime nine times.

Noah was already there, sitting on the tailgate of his faded blue pickup truck.

"Hey. I'm glad you guys came," Noah said as he walked up to them.

Clare gazed at him. She briefly noticed how good he looked in his black jacket and jeans, hands in his pockets.

"Hey, yeah," Clare replied. "I just need to let my parents know I made it safely." She pulled out her phone and FaceTimed her mom's cell. Her parent's faces appeared on the screen. "Hey, Mom. Hey, Dad. Here we are." She panned the phone around, showing them the location—Noah and Caitlin in the background, smiling and waving.

"Okay, honey! Thanks for checking in!" they called.

"Okay. I'll text you before I'm on my way home, k?"

"Sounds good! Love you!" Her parents' faces beamed back at her.

Clare clicked her phone off and shoved it into her pocket.

"Parents, ya know," Clare said to Noah.

"I think it's nice," he replied, shrugging.

Despite the friendly rapport, Clare felt a bit uneasy. A brisk breeze was blowing through the turning oak trees. She cast her eyes across the headstones in front of her as she recalled the faces of the demons as they chased her across the softball diamond. She shivered.

"So, the cemetery, huh?" Caitlin said to Noah, fidgeting. "Romantic." A crow's caw pierced the night air. Then an owl swooped out of a nearby tree diving close to the trio standing near the fence. "Oookay," she said as she pulled her hood over her head.

Clare snickered a little. "Caitlin isn't the biggest fan of flying things. Or crawling things...or...really walking and breathing things of any kind."

"That is not true! I'm fine with people! And dogs!...some of them. It's just that...animals are completely unpredictable."

"Cait, remember that time we built a fort under your parents' desk, and that spider fell down and landed on your shoulder, and you freaked out and stood up, smacking your head and passing out." Clare laughed to herself.

"Yeah, I kind of remember. That's probably what caused it, thank you very much!" Caitlin retorted, smiling but shivering as she apparently shook off the ick feeling she had at the memory.

At that moment, a handful of bats flitted through the branches of the large tree that hovered above them. One dove near the truck, narrowly missing the girls' heads.

"So! If it's okay with you all, I will wait in the truck!" Caitlin hopped up into the passenger seat of Noah's vehicle.

"Caitlin!" Clare yelled, "C'mon!" *Sure. Not afraid of demons but a bat terrifies her. Sheesh.*

"Yeah, no. I'm good!" Caitlin nodded enthusiastically from behind the glass window while giving two thumbs up.

Clare rolled her head to the side and shrugged at Noah, smirking awkwardly.

"That's okay. I was hoping we would have a minute to talk alone anyway," Noah said as he pushed open the chain-link gate.

It creaked in resistance, clanking shut behind them.

They walked down the long, red, gravel path. Granite headstones glistened in the moonlight. Clare scanned the yard remembering the day they buried Ethan. Her heart clenched. His grave was over the knoll next to the large, orange-leafed maple tree.

Chills ran down her arms.

Her hair whipped in the wind, choking around her neck.

Noah continued to lead her across the damp grass, weaving between grave markers before stopping in front of a chalky headstone with a picture of an angel carved into it. It read, 'Sharon A. Bradley 1963-2020.' Noah looked down at Clare. "Clare, I'd like you to meet my mom."

Shocked, Clare took a step back before gazing up at Noah. She studied the headstone and then Noah's eyes. He was somber but steady.

"Oh...Noah...I'm sorry," she said before pausing. "I'm so sorry. I don't know what to say."

"You don't have to say anything. I just wanted to show you...I wanted you to know...that you're not alone. I know you lost your brother last year in that car accident. My sister, Ava, was devastated. Her entire class was, really. A month after that happened, my mom got really sick. We thought it was just a cold, but she had a cough that wouldn't go away. The night that she died, she held my hand and made me promise that I wouldn't lose hope. She made me promise to keep the faith. You see, she knew. She knew those last few days that she wouldn't make it. But she was so fearless. As I was growing up, she would always say to me, 'Noah, remember, death is not the worst thing. What's the worst thing, honey?' And I would reply, 'to die without Christ, Mom.' At the time,

I was annoyed with her always prompting me like that. But she knew she wouldn't be here forever and that I wouldn't either. None of us get out alive, Clare. Fearing death is understandable—to fear the pain and the sadness of missing our loved ones. But death is not the end. She made sure I knew that. It's only the beginning."

"How do you *know* that, though? How are you so sure that this hole in the ground isn't the end?" Clare pushed.

Noah didn't appear fazed. His jaw was set and eyes were intent. "I know because my hope is in the Lord. In John 10:27–28, Jesus says, 'My sheep hear my voice; I know them, and they follow me. I give them eternal life, and they shall never perish. No one can take them out of my hand.' Did you read any sections in the book I dropped off? Thousands of people have clinically died but were resuscitated and experienced heaven and have come back to tell about it. Thousands, Clare! Our life here is only a shadow of what we have to look forward to."

"Why did you have to bring me here to tell me this?" Clare asked.

"Because I wanted to show you something else. That day—the day Nikki threw your sunglasses into the garbage bin—I saw what happened and felt bad for you. I took them out, and when you ran out of the building, I decided to hold on to them until the next time I saw you. But that afternoon, I came here. I come here often to pray and talk to my mom when I miss her. I put on the glasses, Clare. Did you bring them?"

"Yeah." She pulled them out of her sweatshirt pocket.

"Put them on."

"I don't know, Noah. I'm not sure I want to see what's creeping around this place."

"Put them on, Clare. Trust me."

She raised the glasses to her face and gasped at what she saw. At every single gravestone was a radiant flaming form, no two the same.

Clare immediately took off at a run. She wove between the headstones, down the path, over the small hill to Ethan's grave.

Standing guard like a warrior, there was the most beautiful creature Clare had ever seen.

Panting, Noah joined her side.

"What are they doing here?" she asked Noah.

"I think they're standing guard. Although I think some are mourning. See over there?" He gestured to a large black obelisk-type headstone.

Clare turned to look. Next to it, an angel was hunched over. She couldn't see tears, but she could swear that it was sobbing. "I think that angel was guarding a soul that was lost," Noah explained.

"What are they waiting for?"

"I figure they're waiting for the final judgment when Jesus returns, and we rise from the dead to be in heaven with God or in hell—forever."

"I assumed this place would be crawling with demons," Clare replied.

"I did too, actually. But it makes sense. This is a Catholic cemetery. It's holy ground. Demons can't occupy spaces dedicated to God."

"Huh. Yeah." Clare thought back to how they couldn't follow her into the church the other night. "Noah...if demons are real...and angels are real...then heaven and hell are real too, aren't they?"

"Yeah. I'm positive they are. Even before I saw the angels and demons with the glasses, I knew. You've read the Bible, Clare, so you should know too."

"I've never read the Bible."

"Yeah, okay, maybe you've never sat down and read it from start to finish, but you're in Mass every week with your family, right?"

"Yeah, so...?"

"Yeah, so...if you've been in Mass every week for the last three years, you will have heard most of the Bible spoken to you, not to mention that nearly seventy-five percent of the liturgy of the Mass is a direct quote from the Bible."

137

"What?"

"Yeah, for real. So, I know you've heard that none of us are 'mere mortals,' as C.S. Lewis put it. We are body and soul. And we were created to live forever. So after we die, we're going somewhere for the rest of eternity—whether that somewhere is heaven or hell is entirely up to us."

"That's...kind of a lot of pressure," Clare said.

"Yeah, it is. It's the most important choice we will make here on earth. Before I was confirmed two years ago, when the priest signed a cross on my forehead with the blessed oil, I knew. I knew that nothing else mattered if Christ wasn't truly King. And from then on, I've dedicated my life to Him. Now I will fight to the death before I renounce my faith in Jesus Christ."

"Fight to the death...like a warrior?"

"Yeah, a warrior for Truth."

"That's commitment, Noah," Clare said. "I wish I felt that sure."

"Read more, Clare. If you have questions, search until you find the answers. Because there are answers to be found."

"I read one of the sections you highlighted in that book," Clare began, "about a girl who died clinically – where she went to heaven and felt more alive than ever. Your mom...and Ethan...they're at peace now...right?"

"My mom lived her life for Christ. She sacrificed every day for the people she loved in His name. She knew what it meant to love, and she did it with joy. She wasn't perfect, but she strived to live in the Truth, and when she made mistakes, she went out of her way to make things right. I didn't know Ethan. But my sister said he always stood up for people that were getting made fun of and that he was the most loyal friend a person could hope for. God is a merciful Father who loves His children, so I have to believe that my mom and Ethan are more at peace now than we are here on earth, Clare."

"Clare?! Noah?!" Caitlin's distressed shrieks emanated from the direction of Noah's pickup truck.

"Oh! Caitlin! I should get back." Clare glanced at her phone to check the time.

"Hey, Clare," Noah began, "do you think we could meet up again? Like at the library for after-study tomorrow? I'd love to hear more about the glasses."

"Yeah," Clare said. "I'd like that. I just found them recently, over at the old mill. But we can talk about it more tomorrow. Thank you...for telling me about your mom. It is really nice to...know I'm not the only one."

They smiled at each other before Clare slow-jogged back towards the truck.

The windows were fogged up. Clare tapped on the glass to get Caitlin's attention. A little frightened squeal came from inside. She wiped the damp off the window with the sleeve of her shirt and, seeing Clare's face, rolled it down. "What took you so long!? Can we go now? I'm freezing, and there's a spider in here!"

Clare laughed, waved to Noah, and texted her parents that she was on her way home.

"I tell you, my friends, do not be afraid of those who kill the body but after that can do no more. I shall show you whom to fear. Be afraid of the one who after killing has the power to cast into Gehenna; yes, I tell you, be afraid of that one."
Luke 12:4-5

8
The Assignment

The following morning rain was drizzling out of thick gray clouds coating the windows with a heavy mist. Fall had arrived.

Still conscious of the demonic presence around her, Clare wanted to wear the glasses more often. Still, she was not yet prepared to face the reality that the demons could be there with her—in her own home.

She went to the garage to retrieve her bike, pulled her rain jacket hood over her head, put the glasses on, and headed toward school.

As she approached, students were jogging into school to get out of the chill that was in the air.

Clare slid the glasses over her eyes, despite the gloomy weather. She was determined to face the demons that seemed to be most active at the school—probably because there were so many people...and so many temptations.

She recalled her previous conversation with Caitlin in the library. She knew that if she had faith she needn't fear... But what did that look like? She wasn't sure.

Clare rode her bike up to the bike rack. As she was chaining it up, a dark blue sedan pulled up to the school, splashing aggressively through puddles and stopping fast.

Clare looked up. It was Nikki's dad's car. The people in the front seats were shouting at each other. Demons were swarming the vehicle. It was difficult to see what was going on inside with the rain-soaked windshield, but whoever was in the car wasn't happy.

Arms were flailing.

Then the door swung open.

A mess of Nikki spilled out. "Don't forget your

backpack, you little twit!" Nikki's father shouted from the driver's side as an open bag came flying out of the car onto the sidewalk, landing next to Nikki's feet.

Nikki scrambled to pick it up, glancing over at Clare. "What are you looking at?" she hissed. At that moment, a demon passed through her. It even seemed for a moment to inhabit her.

The demon at Nikki's side didn't seem to be attacking her as much as it appeared to be her companion.

I guess the apple doesn't fall far. Clare locked up her bike and ran into the school building.

The sound of hundreds of wet shoes squeaked across the floor. Nikki was at her locker. She clutched her open backpack in one hand and an arm full of books in the other. As she struggled to open her locker, she dropped her folder, and papers spilled onto the damp floor. Clare instinctively bent down to help, picking up a notebook that had flopped open.

Nikki snatched it from her hands viciously. "What do you think you're doing, you little twit? Don't you dare touch my stuff."

"I was just trying to help," Clare explained.

"Yeah, well, maybe you should go help someone that actually needs it, like one of your pathetic little 'friends.' " She gestured with her chin towards Caitlin and Noah, who stood together at the other end of the hall.

"Like I said, Nikki, I was just trying to help. It won't happen again," Clare answered as she turned and walked toward Caitlin and Noah.

A tall, slender blonde strode down the hall towards them. She looked like the type of middle-aged woman who would still get carded when she bought cough syrup. Her golden, shoulder-length waves were impeccable, and her fitted pencil skirt was expertly pressed. She was youthful and stunning, but the severe look on her pursed lips said she wasn't someone to take lightly.

"Mom!" Nikki said, startled, "what are you doing here?"

"I told you last night that I had a meeting this morning with Principal Dunham to change the homecoming dance location from that horrid gymnasium to the bank's private ballroom. Why on earth they think it's acceptable to host a gathering in that wreck is beyond me." As if seeing her daughter for the first time, she shrieked, "Nicole! What in the...look at your hair!" The rain had exhausted Nikki's usually voluminous waves to water-logged locks. "Look at you! You're disgusting! Get in that bathroom and take care of that right now, young lady, before someone sees you! There are cell phones everywhere!" She tugged at Nikki's jacket collar, straightening it. Before she turned to go, she glanced back at her little girl. "There is no room for mistakes, Nicole."

Nikki said nothing but set her things in her locker and walked toward the bathroom. Her mother turned, a shining gold clutch tucked under her arm just so, and walked, with perfection, to the doors.

Clare recalled her own mother, how she used to drop her off and blow her kisses before she would drive away. Embarrassing but sweet. A feeling of gratitude and pity rose in her, and suddenly, Nikki didn't seem so strong and powerful anymore. Now she just looked...human.

✝

Clare, Caitlin, and Noah entered the history room just before the bell sounded. Students quieted down and took their seats as Mr. Schwab's voice rang out, "Attention, class! I know you have all been thrilled with our previous studies of ancient Egyptian hygiene, but we're taking a more local look at history in the coming week. In fact, very local. Your assignment for the weekend—" At this, groans filled the room. There was nothing worse than a project assigned on a Friday.

"Quiet down, quiet down. This should be more fun than it is work, class! Your assignment for the weekend is to research the history of your local community. Now, we all know that Newhill was founded as a mill town, but I want you to dig deep. On Monday, when you present your three-page essay to the class, I expect to hear things about this small town that I've never heard before! Now turn to page 112 of your textbooks. We will be studying how living locally makes a difference."

The class opened their books and flipped through the pages. Clare and Caitlin exchanged glances. As annoying as it was to get homework like this for the weekend, it would be a great excuse to get together and investigate the history of the mill; maybe some research could help shine some light on where these glasses could have come from and why she found them at the mill in the first place.

Clare carefully tore a small square of paper off the corner of her notebook page and wrote:

Partners? After-study tonight?

Caitlin took the note from Clare slyly, unfolding it under her desk, and scribbled her response:

Yes and Yes!

She passed the note back to Clare with a closed fist.

The rest of the school day morning passed uneventfully. Clare and Caitlin were made partners in Science. They argued over who had to slice the frog open and who got to take the notes. Caitlin won the deciding game of Rock Paper Scissors. The smell of pickled flesh and formaldehyde permeated the air as Clare took the scalpel.

At lunch, the girls sat together, eating cheesy mashed potatoes, the only truly delicious thing on the school menu, laughing and sharing thoughts about Noah and why he wanted to meet Clare in after-study that afternoon.

"He loves you, he loves you not." Caitlin was pulling grapes one by one off their stems and tossing them at Clare.

Clare snickered. "He probably just wants to find out more about the glasses."

"I don't know. From what I saw, he's got a thing for you," Caitlin replied, lobbing the last grape in Clare's lap.

"Really? How much could you see from Noah's truck, Cait? Was the back of his head really that informative?" Clare replied, smirking. She tossed the grape back at Caitlin, hitting her directly between the eyes. The girls burst into laughter.

It felt for a moment as if Clare had gone back in time to before the pain of losing Ethan.

The girls were so engrossed in their chat that they didn't even notice Nikki, Elise, and a handful of other girls approaching them. The girls—the entire Cheer squad, actually—walked together to the end of Clare's table like an army brigade preparing for combat.

"Two losers make a match," Nikki jeered.

This isn't going to be good...

Nikki then turned around, getting the whole room's attention before the troupe began to clap, then yell in unison, "Stop it! Stop it! Get away from them! Get away from them!" Then every girl but Nikki dramatically fell to the floor in a mocking display.

Elise stood on a nearby table and recorded the whole act on her phone.

Did they really just reenact that horrific day on the softball field? Why won't she just leave me alone?! Clare's face flushed red with humiliation and fury as she stood up and ran from the lunchroom.

Clare sat on the cool, grimy floor of the girl's bathroom, face in her knees. She heard the creak of the door as it opened.

"Clare?" Caitlin's voice echoed off the tiled walls.

"It was easier before I ever tried to be one of them," Clare choked from the other side of the bathroom stall. "Before, she hardly seemed to notice me. Now it's like I'm the new football to kick around. Why does she hate me so much?"

"I don't think she actually hates you, Clare. I think she actually hates herself, or her life at least."

"Yeah, well, it's not fair."

"Whoever said it is supposed to be?" Caitlin retorted.

"This morning I saw her...Nikki. She was getting out of her dad's car...and her dad was just screaming at her. At that moment, I actually felt sorry for her. And when she dropped her stuff in the hall this morning, I tried to help her, and she practically bit my head off."

"To be humiliated is her worst fear," Caitlin explained, "and she would rather die than be seen as weak."

"Is kindness a weakness? Why not just be kind, for like a minute?!"

"I think she does see kindness as weakness. Here, c'mon." Caitlin took Clare's hand, helping her to her feet. "It's going to be okay. We're in this together."

✝

In the halls after their next class, kids were laughing at their screens. A red-headed boy Clare recognized as a freshman named Will looked up at Clare and Caitlin and snickered. He jabbed the girl next to him in the ribs and pointed toward them.

Clare reached into her pocket and pulled out

her phone. She opened TikTok to see a featured video of herself from lunch, running red-faced from the lunch table like a little girl.

Her knees buckled.

Her heart pounded in her chest.

The judgmental faces surrounded her, but she took a deep breath and straightened her shoulders.

"You know what, forget this," she said to Caitlin. "If what you've said is true, and our identities are in the Lord, why am I trying to prove myself to all these people? Why is what they think so important?"

She opened Settings and paused, her forefinger hovering over the red button, 'deactivate account.' She inhaled, lifting her heart to God in a brief prayer, and clicked it.

"Whoa," Caitlin said. "I feel like I just witnessed a miracle. I've never seen anyone do that before. How's it feel?"

"It feels...liberating." Clare clicked off her phone and slid it into her back pocket.

*"For the weapons of our warfare are not of the flesh
but have divine power to destroy strongholds."*
2 Corinthians 10:4

9
Too Late

As the last bell rang for the day, indicating weekend freedom for the students of Jefferson High, Caitlin and Clare were only beginning their studies. They pulled open the doors to the school library. After-study was only popular before midterms and final exams. Aside from the librarian, only a few students could be spotted throughout the vast, book-lined room. The sound of pencils scratching and the click of the database computer were the only sounds that could be heard echoing off the hard plaster walls.

"It's too quiet in here," Clare whispered to Caitlin. "Let's find a seat where they won't all hear us talking about...ya know."

"Yeah, good call. There's a table down there to the right behind the ancient archeology section. No one ever goes down there. C'mon," Caitlin responded, gesturing with a wave of her hand.

"But how will Noah find us?" Clare asked.

"He doesn't have to," Caitlin stated as she rounded the corner of the towering stacks of dust-laden books. "He's already here."

Noah was seated at the small square pedestal table, books open before him, scribbling notes across lined paper. He looked up at them and smiled.

The girls responded with grins and pulled up seats next to him.

"So, where did you get these glasses, anyway?" Noah's directness broke the silence.

To the best of her memory, Clare recounted to him the timing and location of where she had found the mysterious glasses. She commented on how odd it had been. She had never been beyond the mill gate before, and how strange it was that on that night, they were there.

"God works in mysterious ways," he replied, shrugging his shoulders.

"You could say that," Clare replied.

They spent the next few hours digging through journal after journal, learning all they could of the history of Newhill and the paper industry that put it on the map. Maybe something here could explain why enchanted aviators would be in a place like the old mill.

One book became two, and two became twelve, and before they knew it, the three students couldn't even be seen behind the growing mountain of books and journals.

"Check out this one!" Noah pushed yet another book toward Clare. "It says here that since the early 1900s, the local paper mill had produced millions of tons of paper. The original mill building was located where it still is along the river because they needed the water to power, not just the mill itself but the whole town!

"Newhill went from a town of a couple hundred to twenty thousand in just a decade because so many jobs were available when the mill opened. The way it sounds, everything in this town originally depended upon the success of this industry.

"Everything was going great until the mill was purchased in 1976 by a foreign investor. At that time, it was worth just under a billion dollars!

"But that's when it looks like things really began to go downhill. Apparently, some dirty dealings caused the mill to close for good. It says here that Chem Com manager Ronald Berkely was arrested for embezzling three and a half million dollars from the mill around that time."

"Where's Chem Com?" Clare asked.

"I think that's that chemical factory down the road surrounded by train tracks and barbed wire high-fence," Noah replied, gesturing with his head to the West. "It was believed that he was working with someone inside the mill to siphon funds. Coincidentally, when Berkely was arrested, the current CEO of the mill disappeared, leaving a wife and child behind. He was never heard from again, and charges were never filed. Still, the local authorities strongly believe there was a connection."

Caitlin absentmindedly twisted a coil of her hair. "So, basically, Newhill was founded on the paper industry, and the entire wealth of the city depended on it. So, practically the whole town was affected when the mill shut down?"

"Yeah," Noah replied, "just below this article is an opinion column. A guy named Zachary O'Donnell wrote in because he was seeking justice for his wife. He was a mill employee, and after the mill unexpectedly closed its doors, he lost his health insurance. He was unable to pay for her cancer treatment. She died three weeks later."

"Whoa. That was a lot to take in," Clare responded. "So because of the selfishness and greed of a couple people, hundreds lost their jobs, families suffered, and someone actually died?"

"Yup," Noah said matter-of-factly. "Want to hear something even more bizarre?"

"There's more?!" Caitlin said, "How does it get worse than that?"

Noah passed an enormous open newspaper over to the girls. "So this is where it gets interesting. The same year the mill closed down, there was a rash of church burglaries. Here it actually shows a map of each of the six vandalized and robbed churches. The churches affected fell into a perfect 66-mile radius, with Newhill being the exact center. I mean... that's just too weird to be a coincidence, right?"

"Okay, yeah, that's weird," Clare responded. Both of the girls leaned in to examine the photos on the newspaper page. There was a picture of each one of the burglarized churches.

"Hey! There's St. Anne's!" Caitlin exclaimed.

On page A2, front and center was a photo of a priest standing in front of the church. Below was a description: "Father Grayson reports that one solid gold chalice and seven holy items had been stolen from the nave and rectory of Newhill's Saint Anne's."

"But what does this have to do with the mill closure?" Clare asked.

Noah cleared his throat. "Chem Com manager Ronald Berkely, the guy arrested for stealing money from the paper mill, was also incriminated in the church burglaries. When he was arrested for embezzlement, they took his fingerprints. His fingerprints matched the ones found on the tabernacle in Saint Anne's."

"That doesn't seem that weird, though..." Clare scrunched her face.

Noah leaned forward. "It's weird when only the priest should ever open and close the tabernacle door and when Ronald Berkely claimed to be on vacation in the Bahamas that week."

"Okay, yeah, that is suspicious," Clare conceded.

"And a second set of fingerprints was also found on the tabernacle. They checked the prints against all of the altar servers and priests in the diocese. They never found a match."

Caitlin pulled the newspaper over to inspect it closer. "Though, none of this explains where the glasses might have come from. Or what this inverted 'V' logo could mean. And some of it sounds like it's straight out of a movie."

"Yeah. I think the only way we'll find out more about the glasses is to actually go to the mill ourselves and look for answers," Clare responded.

Caitlin suddenly stood up. "I forgot! I really need to finish my Science project tonight. It's due on Monday. And I want to have enough time to go to your game tomorrow, Clare. I'm building a scale model of the solar system with full rotation and everything!"

"Nice!" Clare replied. "But you don't have to come to the game if you don't have time. I won't be playing in it tomorrow anyway. I'm benched—for leaving practice early last week. Apparently, running from demons doesn't count as an excused absence." Clare smirked.

"Well, I'm coming anyway," Caitlin said. "That's what friends are for."

"I'd like to come, too, if that's okay," Noah added.

Clare nodded to Noah and exclaimed, "Hey! How about after the game tomorrow, we ride together to the place where I found the glasses in the first place?"

They nodded in agreement and waved goodbye to Caitlin.

Clare and Noah sat next to each other for the next couple of hours, poring over journal after journal, searching for anything tracing back to the inverted 'V' logo. But they turned up nothing. Noah shifted in his seat, and Clare abruptly became aware of her close proximity to the handsome boy. She reached for a highlighter on the table, and her hand grazed across his for a moment. "Sorry!" She scooted her chair away from him a bit.

Suddenly, there was a loud mechanical clunk, two clicks, and a low *hummmmmmm*.

The lights went out.

The entire library—the entire school—powered down. Clare instinctively grabbed Noah's hand but quickly thought twice about it. Before she could retract it, he squeezed it in response and whispered, "Clare, it's okay. They must not have realized we were still here. C'mon, grab your things. They probably haven't locked the doors yet."

Clare tapped on her cell phone flashlight and shoved her pen and notebooks into her backpack. She stood up and at once felt her throat tighten. "Noah...do you feel that?"

A cold gust of wind rushed into the room, sending chills down her spine.

"Let's go," he replied firmly.

They grabbed their backpacks and threw them over their shoulders in tandem.

Their shoes squeaked across the cold tile

floor, sending echoes down the corridor.

The shadows cast by their swinging cell phones were eerily large and angular.

They knew they were alone but didn't feel it. The reflections of their silhouettes bounced off every reflective surface, making them feel as though they were surrounded by crowds of hazy, rippling figures.

They pushed through the library doors that clanked closed behind them. The seemingly endless locker-lined halls reached out to their left and their right. Clare veered one way and Noah to the other. "This way!" They both insisted to each other.

"It'll be faster to go down past the front office and out the front doors!" Clare said.

"Yeah, but those will be locked for sure. They chain them from the inside. Let's try the side doors," Noah replied.

Clare joined Noah's side, realizing he was probably right. They jogged down the hallway past dark classroom after dark classroom. After a few minutes—which felt like an eternity—they reached the West Wing exit only to find the double doors to be chained shut. "We're locked in!" Clare shrieked.

Real panic was now beginning to set in.

The moonlight shone in from the windows onto the floor in front of them. BAM! The cold wind they thought they had outrun now blew, slamming a classroom door shut just down the hall from where they stood.

"Noah?!" Clare turned to face him while feeling for the glasses in her sweatshirt pocket. "Did I tell you that the demons know I can see them?"

"No. You didn't mention that," Noah replied, standing, feet firmly planted in the direction of the noise.

Clare slid the glasses onto her face and turned to look. A legion of demons was swarming into the hall from every classroom. "Noah?!" Clare turned her body into him, grasping his t-shirt in her hands, and buried her face in his chest.

The demons rushed upon them, faces gnarled and bodies heaving. Clare felt a cold wind and opened her eyes to see Noah reach into his pocket. He pulled out a braided string of rosary beads and began to pray aloud, "Come, Holy Spirit."

The devils rushed on, growing in size as they approached. While Noah reached around Clare with his left arm to hold her tight, he raised his right hand to his forehead, then to his chest, then completed a sign of the cross, moving his hand from his left shoulder to his right. "Hail Mary, full of grace, the Lord is with you," he prayed. "Blessed are you among women, and blessed is the fruit of your womb, Jesus.  Holy Mary, Mother of God, pray for us sinners, now and at the hour of our death."

At this, the devils reared up like a pack of war horses, flailing and throwing their heads back.

They were repulsed.

Terrified.

Noah continued, "Mary, Queen of heaven, pray for us. Saint Joseph, Terror of Demons, pray for us. Saint Michael the Archangel, pray for us. Sacred Heart of Jesus, have mercy on us. In the name of Jesus Christ, I command you demons, be gone!"

At these words, Clare and Noah sensed the room deflate and then vibrate with a palpable peace.

Clare relaxed her grip from Noah and looked up as she turned around. The demons had vanished.

"They're...they're gone..." Clare whispered, still shaking.

"They're gone," Noah said assuredly.

Silence.

Clare knew at that moment that the strength and peace that Noah had during that dark moment, she wanted for herself.

Bang! A door swung open at the other end of the hall, startling both Noah and Clare, who jumped and separated from each other.

"Hello?!" a deep, husky voice shouted. "Someone down there?!"

"Yeah!" they both yelled in unison.

"We were studying in the library and got locked in!" Noah replied as they both started jogging towards the voice. It was Jeremiah, the school janitor.

"I just locked up and was doin' my rounds outside and thought I saw flashlights in here. Glad I came to check, or you two woulda been in here for the weekend. There's been so much vandalism lately. We keep 'er locked up tight these days."

"Thank you, sir." Noah led Clare out the door behind the uniformed man.

"No, problem. Now you two be more careful from now on."

"Yes, we will," Clare responded, shaking off the nerves and breathing in the cool fresh air.

"Sunglasses in the dark, huh? I'll never understand fashion," the janitor said, shaking his head. He chained the doors shut and turned to walk across the glistening parking lot. As the man walked away, his keys clinking at his side, Clare heard him say, "Haven't seen sunglasses like those since 1965."

"What did he just say?" she asked Noah.

"I don't know. I think he was just talking to himself."

"Hey, Mister!" Clare yelled, running across the parking lot to catch up with the man. "Did you say you've seen sunglasses like these before?"

"What? Huh, yeah. The old mill boss used to wear 'em. Had a pair just like 'em. Even got the Vulcan Volitals logo on 'em and everything."

"Vulcan Volitals? I've never heard of a company called that around here."

"Used to be called Chem Com before it sold to a foreign investor. Huh. Hard to forget a guy like that, my old mill boss. Barking mad, I'm sure. And the cruelest temper. Lucky I was just a young apprentice at the time and didn't have to suffer under him as much as the other mill workers did. Anyways, gotta get goin'. Gonna be late for BINGO at the club."

"K. Thank you!" Clare yelled as she jogged back to Noah's side.

"He said he's seen glasses like these before!" she said to Noah as they walked side by side across the parking lot. "Sir!" she yelled unexpectedly, getting the old man's attention. "What was the mill boss's name?"

"Don't remember the last name, but his first was Devlin."

"Thank you!" she yelled in response. "Noah! Did you hear that?! That's the connection! Vulcan Volitals is Chem Com! That means whoever was responsible for stealing the relics, and gold holy items could be connected to these glasses and the mill after all! We have to go there tomorrow to see if we can figure out more."

"So we searched records all night, just to have the janitor be the source of all sources? Unbelievable."

"Hey. It's just like you said, 'God works in mysterious ways.'" Clare gently nudged Noah's side with her elbow.

They walked across the parking lot together toward the bike rack. Clare fidgeted with her bike lock, rotating in the numbers as she contemplated what had transpired.

"Can I give you a ride home?" Noah asked.

"Yeah, that would be great. Thanks," Clare said, relieved she wouldn't have to ride home alone tonight. Without another word, Noah reached for her bicycle, guided it over to his pickup, and lifted it into the bed of his truck.

They rode together the short ride to Clare's home without speaking a word; they each knew there was nothing they needed to say.

*"Be kind to one another, compassionate, forgiving one
another as God has forgiven you in Christ."*
Ephesians 4:32

10
Friends?

"Hey, Boo! Ready for the big game?!" her father's voice boomed boorishly through the kitchen.

"Dad, I'm benched, remember?"

"Yeah, mom did mention that."

"It's all right, though. I'm going to support my team and be there to help in whatever ways Coach Rhonda will allow."

"That's the spirit, kiddo." Her father squeezed her shoulder and took his coffee to the living room.

"Wow, honey," her mom began, "I'm really proud of you. That's a very mature perspective. Where did this come from?"

"I guess I just realized all of us have choices. I've been trying to do things my way for a while now, and it didn't work out so hot. So, I'm going to try to do things differently from now on."

"Well, knock me off my socks and call me Nancy," her mother said, leaning back with her hands on her hips. "Clare. I'm so proud of you. I don't really know where all of this 'new you' stuff is coming from, but I have to say, I'm thrilled to see it."

"I'm going to go get ready for the game." Clare hopped off the kitchen counter stool and then paused briefly before turning around. "I love you, Mom."

As Clare walked toward the stairs, her mom replied, "I love you more," while blowing her a kiss.

Clare caught it mid-air and placed it on her cheek.

✝

At noon the Thomson family piled into their car and drove to the softball game, arriving just on time. The sun was high in the sky, and the stands were packed. "I want popcorn!" James exclaimed, running immediately towards the concession stand, his parents trailing behind him.

Clare jogged to the dugout where her team readied themselves, each with their own personal 'get pumped' routine. A girl named Gina was jumping up and down while slamming a ball into her glove every other hop. Another girl did lunges. Smalls sat on the bench, shoveling grape bubblegum into her mouth. Clare quietly sat down, waiting for the greetings or jeers, but none came. No one smiled at her. No one glared. It was as if she was invisible. She got up and paced a bit before going over to Coach. "Anything I can do?"

"Well, you can show up on time for one thing and stay for the entire game. You've shown up. Now let's see if you can make it through to the handshakes at the end, huh. This may be the last game of the season, Thomson. I hope next year you come with a new commitment."

"You got it, Coach," Clare replied. The sting in Coach's tone was brutal, but she knew she wouldn't get anywhere with her team or Coach if she let it get to her. She sat back down on the bench and waited for the game to start.

Being benched didn't keep her from joining the other girls on the team for warm-ups. Once she was out on the field, her nerves calmed. That was, until she noticed Noah in the stands grinning at her and clapping. He was seated next to Caitlin and another boy she recognized from school. Instantly butterflies took flight in her guts.

The national anthem came over the loudspeaker, and Clare jogged with her team back to the dugout.

The innings went three up, three down, one at a time until the opposing team made a run and took the lead. Clare encouraged her teammates with a cheer as each took the base. And Caitlin encouraged Clare with a smile every so often from the stands.

Although the Jefferson High Eagles put up a fight, their team lost.

Clare got up with the rest of her exhausted teammates. She took the field and congratulated the other team on their win. Back at the dugout, her coach congratulated her on making it through the game.

"You ready?!" Caitlin chimed, her face stuck up next to the dugouts' chain-link fence.

"Almost. Let me change clothes, okay, and then we can head out."

"Excellent cheering today." Noah approached her, beaming.

"Thanks. I was pretty solid, if I do say so myself," Clare replied. "I think I even deserve an ice cream," she said, smirking. "I just need to change, and then we can go."

Clare, Caitlin, and Noah walked together towards the bathrooms, a solitary cement block building just behind the concession stand. As they rounded the corner, they saw a tall, dark-haired teen boy raising his hands violently and shouting. A thin young woman stood in front of him with her hands held up to her face, clearly distraught. Clare strained to hear but couldn't make out what he was saying.

"Isn't that Finn?" Noah said.

"Yeah, and that's Elise," Clare replied.

Just then, Finn shouted again and then stormed away. With tears streaming down her face, Elise backed up to the cold block building wall and slumped to the ground, sobbing.

"Should we go over there?" Caitlin whispered to Clare.

"After everything she's done to us? Are you kidding?" Clare's lip curled at the thought.

"I don't know. It looks pretty bad, Clare. Even Elise has feelings, I suppose," Caitlin replied, taking a step forward and glancing back at Clare.

Before Clare could decide whether or not to act, Noah strode forward. "Are you okay?" he asked, looking down at her. Elise lifted her chin, wiped her eyes, and adjusted herself uncomfortably on the ground.

"Just leave me alone," she said. Her mascara was running down her cheeks.

Finally realizing that to help was clearly the right thing to do, Clare walked up to Noah. "Can you give us a minute?" she asked.

Noah took the cue and touched Caitlin on the shoulder, guiding her a few steps down the sidewalk so that Clare and Elise could have some privacy.

"I told you to leave me alone." Elise hugged her knees tighter as Clare approached.

"Elise, you look scared. Finn seemed really upset. What's going on?"

"Nothing. You wouldn't understand."

"I might," Clare said as she sat down on the rough, cold concrete next to Elise.

"I just want things to go back to normal."

"I know the feeling..." Clare responded. "I mean...I don't know exactly how you feel...but I know the feeling of wanting to go back in time. Undo it. Start over."

"Yeah, undo it...start over. That's what I'll do." Elise promptly stood up and brushed off her jeans with her hands. "Thanks." She sniffed hard and hustled across the parking lot. Clare saw Caitlin and Noah stop her as she was about to pass. Caitlin had taken Elise's hand and said something to her. Noah had his back to Clare but may have said something as well.

Clare rushed over to join the other two as Elise walked briskly away.

"What did you say to her?" Caitlin asked. "Whatever it was, it must have helped."

"I'm not really sure. All I said was that I understand the feeling of wanting to undo bad things that happen—wanting to start over." Clare shrugged. "What did you say to her?"

"I just invited her to church with us tomorrow. I said that there is help there...if she needed it. I've just never seen Elise cry before. I figured it must be pretty bad if she's willing to be seen in public acting like that."

"Huh. Elise in church. That would be something," Clare said in a doubtful tone. "So, should we get going then?"

"You haven't even gotten your much-deserved ice cream," Noah interjected. "That bench couldn't have kept itself warm." He smirked at Clare. "Seriously, though, your cheering was top-notch."

They laughed and got their refreshments. After Clare changed, they headed to Noah's truck.

Clouds were growing on the horizon.

"Do not fear: I am with you; do not be anxious: I am your God. I will strengthen you, I will help you, I will uphold you with my victorious right hand."
Isaiah 41:10

11
Research

They rode together the short ride down to the abandoned mill and parked along the sidewalk. The looming structures didn't look so frightening in the daylight, but they were nonetheless intimidating. "So..." Caitlin began, "are we even allowed to go in here?"

"Technically, no..." Noah replied, "but it's for the sake of research." He shrugged.

"It's necessary. We'll get in and get out as fast as we can. It'll be all right." Clare assured her.

"But we do need to be careful. The police do patrol the place every so often to keep the riff-raff out," Noah added.

"I'm pretty sure we're the riff-raff today, guys," Caitlin said, looking around uneasily.

"It's gonna be okay, Cait. C'mon." Clare opened the truck door and hopped out.

It was day, but inside the mill, it was night black.

Then, it began to rain.

The echoes from each drop were amplified in the three-story, cavernous space.

As Clare, Caitlin and Noah wandered deep inside, they had to be careful to step clear of the large pits carved into the cracking concrete floors where large equipment had once been. They ducked under enormous steel beams that jutted out here and there, unpredictably. The whole place smelled of dust and bad dreams.

"Why are we doing this again?" Caitlin asked. Clare had the chills and figured Caitlin must too. She didn't appear to be a big fan of the noise that the large panes of rusted metal siding made as the now-gusting wind blew through.

"Because we need to find answers," Clare replied, hopping over a hula-hoop-sized crater in the damaged concrete floor.

"Oh, yeah." Caitlin paused at the edge of the gap and jumped with two feet to clear it. When she landed, the sound of grit between her rubber soles and the pavement was like sandpaper across a chalkboard.

Rain relentlessly pinged off of the tin roof. Drips were creating pools where the roof panels were cracked. Their postures were growing increasingly tense the further they ventured into the darkness. "Hey! Stop touching me!" Caitlin suddenly yelled out.

"No one's touching you. We're over here!" Clare said from a few paces away.

Caitlin shrieked and scurried to Clare's side. "What if there are people in here? Ya know, squatters..." she whispered as she joined Clare's side.

"I don't know anyone that would want to live in a place like this, Cait. It's the demons that worry me," Clare replied. Although she was desperate for answers to where the glasses might have come from, her nerves were on edge.

"I don't know." Noah glanced around. "No one has worked here for years. Why would demons want to hang around a place with no one to torment?"

"That's true," Clare said, pausing. "But *we're* here now..."

Noah moved closer to the girls. "C'mon. Let's stick together. We could easily get lost. And I have no idea how we'd find each other if we got split up. Remember, it's best if we don't show fear. Have some faith."

"Easy for you to say," Clare muttered as they made their way to a place where a conference room narrowed to a hall.

"Hey. I think we found the offices," Noah said.

They each began shining their cell phone flashlights in every direction, looking for something—anything that could shed light on why the mystery glasses were found here, of all places.

They spent the next few minutes pulling open rusting filing cabinets and discarded binders of building blueprints.

"Hey guys, over here!" Clare suddenly exclaimed. "Down here. I think this must have been the supervisor's office," she said, nudging an old leather desk chair on casters with her foot, "or someone important at least." It was an impressively large office with a stately desk and a view down to the production floor from a large, now broken, window.

"I don't know if important is the right word for whoever's office this was, Clare." Noah paused in the doorway. Across all of the walls and the window looking down to the production floor, in bright red spray paint, were the words "YOU OWE ME!"

The feeling of pins danced down her neck.

"I don't think we should be in here," Caitlin said, turning her flashlight quickly this way and that.

"This is *exactly* where we should be, Cait. This room has to be significant. Hey, check this out!" Clare exclaimed. There, still hanging on the wall, was a picture of a group of men standing near some large machinery. One of them was wearing aviator sunglasses. "It's a framed newspaper article from October 1968. Oh my gosh! You guys! You're not going to believe this!" Clare said, yanking the picture off the wall.

Caitlin and Noah rushed over to join her, their eyes squinting to make out the tiny, printed caption below the image." Caitlin was reading the names of the men one by one as Clare grew impatient.

"And Devlin Thacker!" Clare said, raising her voice to a shouting level. Her words echoed down into the production level through the busted-out glass.

"The one wearing the glasses?" Noah asked.

"Yup!" Clare answered.

"No way! Isn't that Nikki's dad's name?!" Caitlin said.

"Yeah," Clare replied. "But there's no way the guy in this picture could be her dad...he would be like...75 or 80 years old right now."

"No, Clare," Noah said. "Her dad is a junior. This must be her grandfather."

Caitlin, standing with one arm leaning on the large desk in the middle of the room, flipped up the desk placard. It read 'Devlin Thacker-CEO.'

"Unbelievable..." Clare said as she moved to touch the desk.

"Hey! You guys can't be in here!" a stern voice suddenly shouted from down the hall.

A uniformed police officer entered the dark room, shining a flashlight into each of their faces.

"Oh, crap!" Clare shouted. She instinctively took flight, taking advantage of the shadows and diving through an open office door. As the police officer passed, she slipped out behind him and ran. She stumbled and fell flat out on the floor, picked herself up, and hit the stairs running. She heard someone close behind her. Moments later, she burst out onto the production floor.

"We're just researching for our history assignment!" she heard Caitlin's voice chime through the broken window above. Clare knew Caitlin had an uncanny way of accidentally using her innocence to her advantage.

She glanced up at the window. The flashlight shone down on her, reflecting light off her damp, sweaty skin.

Noah then clambered down the stairs.

"C'mon!" she called out to him.

"But what about Caitlin?!" he shouted as he sprinted up to her.

"She'll be fine!" Clare assured him.

They retraced their steps, zig-zagging through the maze of rooms, flying out into the muddled daylight into the downpouring rain.

They jogged together towards Noah's truck.

"Shouldn't we wait for her?" Noah asked, intently gazing in the direction from which they came.

"I don't know. What if they get your license plate number?" Clare replied frantically.

"We can't just leave her here."

"What's the alternative? That we all get in trouble?"

Noah started the engine. "I'm going to pull off to the side. We can watch to make sure she's all right," he said, driving just around the corner and backing into a shadow just right so that they would have a view of the entrance.

A little while later, they watched as the police officer escorted Caitlin out. He held his jacket over her as they walked quickly, side by side, to the squad car. Tears ran down her face as he opened the back door and ushered her in.

"Oh no," Clare uttered.

"This isn't right. We shouldn't have left her there." Noah shook his head.

"I thought she would be right behind me!" Clare replied.

They peered through the rain-speckled windshield as the squad car pulled away from the curb—with their friend inside.

"I have brushed away your offenses like a cloud, your sins like a mist; return to me, for I have redeemed you."
Isaiah 44:22

12
Reconciliation

Clare and Noah sat in silence in Noah's truck outside the mill before Clare dared speak. "She looked pretty upset, huh?"

"I'd say so," Noah replied. He wouldn't make eye contact with her.

"I think I should call her." Clare took out her phone, staring at the blank screen for several moments. She looked up at Noah. He glanced at her and then steadied his eyes straight ahead.

"I'm going to call her," Clare said, more matter-of-factly this time.

She picked up her phone and tapped Cait's contact. The phone rang.

And rang.

And rang.

And rang.

Voicemail.   Clare swiftly tapped the red button, ending the call.

"No answer," she said. "Let's head back to my place. We can talk things over there."

Ten minutes later, they strolled up the sidewalk to Clare's house. The rain was still coming down. They each took a seat in a white wicker chair on the porch.

Clare bent over and set her purse on her knees.   She reached in and pulled out the framed photograph from the mill office.

"You took the picture?!" Noah exclaimed.

"Well...yeah. It didn't seem to really belong to anybody.   And I'm going to return it—when we're done. I didn't get a chance to study it before that officer came in."

Noah leaned in close to Clare. Their heads hovered over the dusty, faded photograph. Clare was so close to Noah that she could smell the aroma of his cologne. She forgot for a moment what she was going to say. *Oh, yeah.* "Noah," she began, "the only person in the photo wearing sunglasses is the one labeled Devlin Thacker. It's too hard to see if there is a logo on them." She squinted.

"Clare. Do you have a magnifying glass or anything?" Noah said, sitting up.

She sat up, pausing to think. "No....hmmmm," she said. "Actually, yes! Just a minute." She pushed through the front door and jogged up the stairs to her room. A moment later she reappeared in front of Noah, holding a black duffle bag. She plunked it down on the porch and knelt next to it. "It's my old bag from camp," she said. "We were given survival packs. I think there's a magnifying glass in here somewhere; we used them to start fires...here!" She rose, a tiny glass circle proudly in hand.

"Sweet!" Noah took it from her. "Clare..." he began softly. Clare moved in close to him.

"No...way," she replied, peering through the lens—her head right next to his.

There, clear as day, on the upper right lens of the aviator sunglasses, perched on the face of Devlin Thacker, Nikki Thacker's grandfather, was a tiny Vulcan Volitals logo.

"Whoa," Clare and Noah uttered in unison.

Clare picked up the sunglasses and held them up next to the picture. Sure enough. They were identical.

"If these are the same glasses...and Devlin Thacker was the man responsible for siphoning millions of dollars to that Vulcan Volitals company and single-handedly shutting down the town's main source of revenue...then Nikki's grandfather was responsible for this town almost ceasing to exist and that man's wife dying." Clare shook her head. "Not to mention he must have been involved with the church burglaries too!"

"We need to go to church. Someone there must have been around when all those crimes were committed," Noah added.

"Let's talk to Father Mike!" Clare said, getting to her feet.

"Father Mike is only in his fifties," Noah said. "He wasn't the pastor when the holy items were taken, Clare. Not to mention he's blind. What are you going to do? Show him the glasses? Ask him if he recognizes the logo?"

Clare hesitated, realizing Noah had a point. "Yeah, I don't know how exactly, but he knew Father Grayson. And he was the pastor of Saint Anne's for almost thirty years! If what happened during that year of the church burglaries was really significant, there's no way Father Grayson wouldn't have informed his successor about it." Clare moved towards the door.

"All right. But Mass starts at 5:00. If we are going to make it in time to talk to him, we better go now," Noah said.

Clare picked up the photo and stuffed it into her purse once more. "But what about Caitlin?"

She had only just repaired her relationship with Cait. She couldn't afford to lose her again.

Noah shrugged. "Well, you tried to call her. What more can we do right now? If we're going to make it, we better hurry."

Clare nodded.

They jogged together back into the rain.

When Noah's truck pulled into the diagonal parking space in front of Saint Anne's, the rain was still coming down hard, spattering the windshield. A few solitary churchgoers were shuffling in under umbrellas.

"Well, what are we waiting for?" Clare asked as they sat in the truck, pausing just a little longer than she was prepared for.

"It's 4:30 now," Noah said.

"Yeah...and?" Clare responded, impatiently tapping her hand on her knee.

"He's hearing confessions now. And from there, he'll begin Mass straight away."

"Well, I guess you'll just have to go to confession then," Clare replied without hesitation.

"I will have to go to confession then? They're *your* glasses. Besides, I just saw him for confession yesterday." Noah crossed his arms.

"Well, maybe we should just talk to him tomorrow then, after Mass."

"Tomorrow, we'll never have the chance. There will be hundreds of churchgoers there. People are always lining up to talk with Father after Mass about schedules, and bathroom sink leaks, and all that stuff. We'll never get him alone," Noah replied.

"Well, I guess it's now or never." Clare opened the truck door. Rain blew in at her, smattering her exposed legs. "I suppose it's actually the perfect time. We will be alone. And what you tell a priest in confession is confidential, so at least he won't be telling anyone about what I tell him. C'mon." She jumped down from the truck and jogged in, Noah close behind.

The noise of the rain pattering down onto the stone steps hushed as the heavy doors banged shut behind them. They stepped into the church and shook the rain off their jackets onto the damp floor. The sudden noise of their entrance echoed loudly in the almost silent sanctuary.

Aside from Charlie, the dog, who was lying down contentedly, only two people were waiting in the line outside the small, wooden-framed nook off the side aisle. A red light shone above it, indicating someone was occupying the confessional.

They took their place in line, Clare in the lead.

They waited patiently in silence as the light above the confessional went from red to green and then back again to red as the next parishioner entered.

One more person, and then it would be Clare's turn.

Clare's stomach suddenly twisted as she was struck with nerves.

She recalled the last time she had been to confession, the Easter before Ethan had died. She hadn't been back since. She remembered the anxious feeling before going in to tell of her sins. She had always felt that way when she would stand in line, even when she was in second grade, the first time. Her mother had consoled her. "Don't worry, honey. Everyone is anxious before they confess the things they have done that have hurt Jesus. But, when you come out, you won't be able to stop smiling. I promise." She recalled her mother's encouraging smile and the fresh feeling she had felt after that first time in confession—like a clean white sheet on a summer afternoon, blowing in the warm breeze.

The light turned green.

It was her turn.

She pulled back the deep blue velvet curtain. She slid into the confessional, kneeling in front of the screen, which seemed at the moment quite silly, considering Father Mike couldn't see her anyway. And she knew he would recognize her voice instantly. Still, the screen was a comfort to her.

"Bless me, Father, for I have sinned," she began. "It's been...around a year and a half...since my last confession." She took a deep breath. She had only gone in to ask him about the sunglasses, but something in her stirred, urging her to speak what needed to be spoken. She bowed her head and closed her eyes. "These are my sins."

She dug deep into her heart, raised it to God, and confessed all of her transgressions.

She told of how she had hurt her friends—especially Caitlin—and her family. The ways she had failed Our Father in heaven and the ways she had failed herself. She told of her thoughts and words, what she had done and what she had failed to do. She told of her doubt and her anger. And after she had nothing more on her conscience, she spoke a heartfelt Act of Contrition, asking for her Father in heaven to have mercy on her. The priest assigned her a penance. Then Clare finally heard the words she had so longed to hear as Jesus, in the voice of Father Mike, said, "My child, thank you for coming to the blessed sacrament of confession today, for laying your mistakes and struggles at the feet of the cross. God, the Father of mercies, through the death and resurrection of his Son has reconciled the world to himself and sent the Holy Spirit among us for the forgiveness of sins; through the ministry of the Church may God give you pardon and peace, and I absolve you from your sins in the name of the Father, and of the Son, and of the Holy Spirit. Amen. You are clean. Go now, and sin no more."

She raised her right hand to her forehead, then to her chest, and then across from her left shoulder to her right, signing herself with a cross.

A wave of peace flooded over her, and a smile grew on her face, just like it had that first time when she was only eight. Her mother had been right. It was impossible not to smile when one felt so new.

She then remembered again what she had come to do. "Father!" she yanked back the screened curtain that separated them. "Father, there's something I need to ask you."

"Clare, what is it?" Father Mike responded sincerely but was clearly startled.

"Do you know anything about these?" She reached around, handing him the pair of sunglasses.

She watched as Father Mike held the glasses, turning them over in his hands. He sat back, appearing to close his eyes, and then, with a start, stood up and set them down quickly on the table next to him. "Where did you get these?" he asked, his forehead wrinkled with concern.

"I found them. At the old mill," Clare replied, reaching over, picking them up off the table. "I was hoping you could help me understand where they might have come from. I read that years ago, some churches around here were robbed."

He took a breath and lowered his voice to a whisper. "Yes. Many precious items were taken from Saint Anne's years ago. And not just from Saint Anne's but from parishes throughout the area. It was a dark time. I don't suppose I should tell you this, but since you already seem to know... When I was made pastor here years ago, I found a letter left to me from Father Grayson. He warned me that there was a man in this town. He could never prove it, but he swore that he was responsible for the theft of a solid gold chalice and several honored relics from this church. The authorities never recovered any of the stolen items. A rumor circulated that the precious metal pieces may have been melted down and repurposed. I was blessed with a charism of the senses. I can feel that these glasses are...powerful. I believe they were made for dark purposes. Please. Be careful."

"Are they evil, Father?" Clare asked, gripping the glasses tighter in her hand.

"Nothing is in itself evil, Clare. It is what we do with our gifts that determines their worth. The choice is yours."

Organ music began, resounding throughout the church, indicating the start of Mass.

"I have to go," Father Mike said. "Remember what I've told you."

"I will, Father. Thank you," Clare replied, rising and exiting the small, dimly-lit space.

The church was now filled with parishioners. The smell of incense spread throughout the air as Noah stood inconspicuously in the side aisle, waiting.

"Put on then, as God's chosen ones, holy and beloved, heartfelt compassion, kindness, humility, gentleness, and patience, bearing with one another and forgiving one another, if one has a grievance against another; as the Lord has forgiven you, so must you also do."
Colossians 3:12-13

13
Regret

As Noah drove Clare back home, she filled him in on what Father had said. The rain had cleared, and after he parked, Noah walked around to open the passenger door for Clare. She stepped out, and he asked, "He could sense it?"

"Apparently. Who knew Father Mike was so fascinating," Clare replied.

They sat down next to each other on the front steps.

"So, he said they were made for dark purposes," Noah repeated Father's words as he sat, hunched over his knees, rubbing his forehead as though he could massage understanding into his brain. "So, the police believe Devlin Thacker was responsible for the mill closing down. And he is directly connected to that Berkely character who was arrested for the thefts of the holy items in all six churches in 1968. And Father Mike believes the holy items taken were melted down...and he can sense that the glasses hold special power. That still doesn't tell us *why* they were made."

"Maybe Devlin used them to exploit weakness—like demons do." Clare shrugged. "Maybe they helped him take advantage of all those people he stole money from."

"If so many holy items were taken, there's no way they were all used to make this one pair of glasses," Noah added.

"Good point," Clare replied. "You think there are more things like this floating around Newhill?"

"I kind of hope not," Noah responded. "This one pair alone has caused us enough trouble already. I don't know, Clare. Maybe if they were really made for dark purposes, we shouldn't be messing around with them." Noah looked down at the glasses that reflected his own concerned face back at him. "Maybe we should turn them in."

"Are you serious? Turn them into who? Umm, excuse me, officer. Here's a pair of sunglasses that shows you an invisible spiritual world. How do you think that's going to go over?" Clare said a little too brusquely.

"Man, Clare. It was just a thought." Noah angled his body away from her slightly.

"All I know is that I just found out something that could downright humiliate Nikki Thacker at school next week when I reveal, in my history report, that her whole family is a fraud whose money came from the destruction of an entire town and even caused a woman to die."

"You're not actually going to use that against her, are you?" Noah asked.

"Why wouldn't I? After what she's put me through? After what she's put Cait through? It's only right!"

A gap of more than a couple inches of porch grew between them at that moment.

Noah shook his head and stood up. "I should get going." He walked down the wooden stairs to the sidewalk. "I guess I'll see you at school on Monday." He strolled to his truck, hands shoved into his pockets.

"Okay. I'll see you tomorrow at church, though, right?" Clare asked, suddenly wishing she had been a little less open about her disgust with Nikki.

"Yeah, I suppose so."

"Okay, bye," Clare replied.

Noah drove off, leaving Clare alone with her thoughts.

✝

"How did everything go with your research today, honey?" Clare's mom asked her at dinner.

"Fine," is all Clare could say.

"Everything all right, Boo?" her father asked, pausing between bites of pork chop.

He gave her a knowing look. Clare realized that her father knew that 'fine' never meant 'fine' with the women in his household. "I don't know. I thought it was going well. But, now I'm not so sure," Clare said.

"Is there anything we can do to help?" he asked.

"Can I be excused? There's something I need to do."

"Sure, hun. Family movie tonight. Seven PM. Don't forget," he said, smiling. "Doctor Seuss and the Who's! You won't want to miss it! I'll make the popcorn!"

Clare smiled at him and rolled her eyes. She grabbed her phone off the kitchen counter and retreated to her bedroom. Tomorrow she wouldn't be allowed access to her phone, so if she was going to repair things with Caitlin, it had to be now.

"Hey, Cait. Everything okay?" she typed into her phone.

...*tap tap tap*... No. She deleted it and tried again.

"Hey, how are you?"

...No. Deleted once again.

"Caitlin...I'm sorry. I don't know what I was thinking. When that cop came in, I was so freaked I just split. I shouldn't have left you like that."

...*tap*. Sent.

A moment later, a bubble with three dots appeared on her screen.

Then they disappeared.

And appeared again.

Then gone.

Clare waited...hoping those dots would transform into words of acceptance—words of forgiveness.

But they didn't.

That night Clare had trouble falling asleep.

I said I was sorry... She turned over in her

bed. *Things had been going so well. And now I'm right back to where I started...alone. Why do I keep hurting people?*

She grabbed a pillow, hugged it tight to her chest, and then picked up her phone, tapping the screen to check for any missed messages.

There were none.

"When you call me, and come and pray to me, I will listen to you. When you look for me, you will find me. Yes, when you seek me with all your heart."
Jeremiah 29:12-13

14
Redeemed

The church bells chimed ten times as Clare and her family settled into their pew.

How quickly things can change.

Just yesterday, I thought things were getting better. Then one stupid choice, well...maybe two stupid choices...okay, so technically three—three stupid choices, and here I am again, friendless and alone.

She had been hoping to sit with Caitlin and Noah at this morning's Mass, but now Noah won't even make eye contact with her, and Caitlin was back to holding her at a distance.

Clare reached into her pocket and slyly tapped on her screen, hoping to see a text from Caitlin, but there weren't any. She silenced her phone and raised her eyes to the crowd of people around her.

There was Noah, sitting between his dad and sister. As she looked at him, the sting from yesterday's conversation swarmed her mind.

A few pews behind him sat Caitlin, her parents, and four sisters, sequentially seated by size next to her. Clare stared intently at her back, hoping that Caitlin might feel it and turn around and smile at her.

Nope.

The music started, and everyone stood. The woody scent of incense filled the air as the bold voices of the congregation sang the opening hymn.

Clare heard the church doors open. She and a few others turned around to see which family was arriving late this week.

No *way*. There, standing at the entrance in a gorgeous salmon-colored dress and cream dress coat, was Elise—somehow appearing even more radiant than ever. She shifted her feet as she glanced around, apparently searching for an empty seat. Then, she walked forward, about halfway down the center aisle, and without bothering to genuflect, slipped into a pew—next to Noah.

Oh, you've got to be kidding me. Jealousy rose like a whale to the surface in Clare's chest.

As the song ended and the opening words were spoken, they all took a seat.

Deacon walked to the pulpit to give the readings as Clare studied Noah's actions. She watched intently as Noah opened a missal and handed it to Elise. Then he leaned over and whispered something in her ear.

He probably never liked me anyway. He was probably only spending time with me because of the stupid glasses. Either way, whatever chance I had is shot to crap now. Look at her! She watched as Elise reached over and touched Noah's arm. *Ugh. Oh, if Finn knew...*

Deacon Mark's voice, loud and clear, echoed through the church, speaking the first reading, 2 Sm 5:1-3 and the second reading, Col 1:12-20 and the Gospel of Luke 23:35-38. But Clare was so distracted by Elise and Noah that she heard none of it.

It wasn't until Father Mike's voice rang over the speakers that Clare's ears noticed. "We are all God's beloved Children, but faith is a relationship. It's not merely a one-time declaration but a commitment to love. A promise to serve. Love is a sacrifice. We are called to suffer in this world as Christ suffered for us on the cross. Being a Christian is not a promise that all will be easy in this life. In fact, it is a promise that it won't." Father added, "They hated Jesus. And they will hate you too. But that is the sacrifice we are called to make. It's a radical choice, but a necessary one if we are to spend our next life in heavenly peace. So, brothers and sisters, forgive others as you have been forgiven. We must make amends for our sins. We can be forgiven of anything as long as we are sorry and ask for forgiveness. Judas made this fatal error. He doubted God's mercy. He despaired and took his own life rather than lay down his pride at the feet of Jesus and beg for forgiveness. As Jesus hung on the cross, dying, two thieves hung on their own crosses, one to each side of him. One wore his sin to the end. The other recognized his need for a savior. This latter thief said to Jesus, 'Remember me as you enter into your kingdom.' And Jesus replied, 'Truly, I say to you today you will be with me in Paradise.' "

"No matter the sin, if you are truly sorry and ask for forgiveness, you will be forgiven. Christ will always forgive you if you turn to Him in humility, with a contrite heart, and repent. You are so loved by your creator that He was willing to suffer a horrific public humiliation and die a most painful death for *you*. *Every* life is *that* precious. So...which thief will you be?"

He paused.

218

The congregation was quiet.

Suddenly, a sob pierced the silence as Elise stood, one of her hands held up to her face, and ran out of the church.

Clare's heart swelled as she realized, at that moment, that faith isn't a burden. It's a gift.

We are *all* loved by God as His children and it is our choice whether we love Him back. God isn't some lofty dictator in the sky. He is our personal Savior and loving Father. And He sent His only son to us from heaven so that we might know the way to sanctification and enjoy a blissful eternal life with God.

If we want to love Him, we need to give ourselves fully to Him—surrender our selfishness and pride—our wants and desires. He wants our whole selves.

He wants me.

James reached out and held Clare's hand as the congregation prayed, "Our Father, who art in heaven, hallowed be thy name thy kingdom come, thy will be done on earth as it is in heaven. Give us this day our daily bread, and forgive us our trespasses." Clare's eyes were still on Noah. At these words, he turned around and looked at Clare as his mouth made the words, "as we forgive those who trespass against us; and lead us not into temptation, but deliver us from evil." He turned back to face the priest, whose hands were held up in prayer below the crucified Christ.

Forgive us our trespasses, as we forgive those who trespass against us... Clare replayed the words in her mind.

Which thief would she be? She needed to choose. And she knew she couldn't wait any longer to decide.

After Mass, Clare weaved between parishioners as they filed out of the church. She peeked between the shifting bodies searching for any sign of Noah. She spotted him and approached eagerly but cautiously. A moment later they were standing face to face in a sea of people, a rock with a river flowing to each side of them—facing against the current.

"I'm sorry," Clare said.

"What? I can't hear you," he replied.

"I'm sorry!" she said too loudly.

People began casting curious glances their way. Clare peered around, suddenly self-conscious.

Noah didn't seem to notice, and Clare didn't want to lose her opportunity, so she continued—this time a little quieter than before, "I'm sorry for being so stupid. And selfish. And

prideful. You were right. Father Mike was right.
I just wanted to say...I'm sorry."

Noah paused, apparently taking it all in.
"Thank you," he replied. Then he smiled at her
and turned to rejoin his family.

Clare wasn't sure what she expected to
happen, but *that* wasn't it. Maybe she thought
it would be like in the movies, where they would
rush towards each other and meet in a
passionate embrace, twirling in circles, lips
locked. Yeah, it *definitely* wasn't that...but she
said what she needed to say. And it seemed
that he accepted her apology. Anyway, that was
huge progress for her! And now, with her
conscience clear, she could focus on what
mattered most—giving herself to God.

✝

When Clare and her family returned home from Mass, she held James' hand and walked him into the house. She tousled his hair as he ran off to play. Clare sat down on the couch.

What am I waiting for? She replayed the last week's events in her mind, thinking about Noah's steadfastness in that horrifying moment at the school. *Remember, bravery isn't the absence of fear but courage despite it.*

Clare's mom stepped into the living room from the kitchen. She was on the phone.

She tipped the phone's microphone back away from her mouth and whispered, "Clare, have you seen James? He was here a minute ago, but now I don't know where he could have gone. Can you go look for him, please?" Clare nodded in reply and got up off the couch. Her mother lifted the receiver back to her face, stepped back into the kitchen, and continued her conversation in a cheery tone.

Clare glanced around the living room and peeked behind the couch. It was James' go-to hide-and-seek spot. "James!" she called out. No response.

She padded up the staircase, pausing briefly to peer back into the living room from the elevated view. Still no little brother. She continued up the stairs.

"James!" she called out. "Ready or not, here I come!" It wasn't unusual for her brother to initiate a game of hide and seek without first recruiting others in the game.

She tiptoed down the hall. The first room was her parents'. She pushed the door open and looked in. It was dark. There was no movement. She continued down the hall, pausing at the next door. It was Ethan's. Although he had been gone for over a year now, his room remained untouched. Sure, their mom had gone through and parted with a few things. However, she couldn't bring herself to remove the photographs that still clung to the walls—dozens of prints, stuck with that blue putty, corners curling up at the edges. Clare stepped into the room. It still smelled of Ethan's cologne. She ran her hand across the antique dresser, letting it settle on a framed photo of Ethan and her. It was her first year at camp. She was so proud. She wore a ribbon she'd won in the archery competition. His arm was around her. They were smiling.

James' little voice broke off her memories.

She could hear him cooing away but couldn't make out his words.

"James!" she called out again. "Are you in my room? How many times have I told you—" her voice trailed off as she pushed open her bedroom door to find her little brother standing on the edge of her bed, both arms outreached.

He was wearing the sunglasses. "James!" she yelled as she lunged, catching him just as he was about to step off the bed.

"Pretty!" he squealed.

She propped him on her hip and tore the glasses off his face.

He immediately started to cry.

"No, no, James!" She caressed his face. Visions of what he could have seen rushed through her mind. If he saw the demons—oh, it was too much to think. She carried him to the door and set him down in the hall. "Mom!" she yelled, "He's up here! I'm sending him down, okay?!" She straightened his shoulders and nudged the sniffing toddler down the hall. "Go be with mom, okay? I'll be down in a bit. I have to deal with something."

She had always been afraid to see what was in her bedroom, so near to her, but she knew she couldn't avoid it any longer. If there was anything here—anything that didn't belong—it had to go. She needed to protect this brother. Ethan had always been there for her. Now it was her turn to do the protecting.

She moved to her dresser top mirror, looking more through herself than at herself. "You can do this." She closed her eyes and slid the glasses onto her face. She took a deep breath and opened her eyes. She saw only her own reflection.

Then in a flash, two demons rushed upon her. Their ugly reflections glistened in her mirror, one to each side of her face, whispering despairing thoughts into her ears. *Who are you to think you can fight darkness? You weakling. You're just a girl. Only human. A child.*

She jumped backward and turned around, flailing her arms for them to get away from her.

She was frantic.

The dark, shadowy forms obscured her view, but she glimpsed a light in the corner of her room. *There!* In the corner, next to her open window, were two angels. *Her* angels. Of course, they were there!

"Why are you just standing there?!" Clare shouted, "Why aren't you helping me?!"

The demons appeared as if they were about to devour her. Then each of the angels raised an arm and pointed directly at Clare.

"Me?! What about me?!" she stammered. "Ohhhhh, ME!" Of course! She stood straight, her feet firmly rooted, and closed her eyes. Then she lifted her heart to God and prayed aloud in a strong and fervent voice, "Angels of God, my guardians dear, to whom God's love commits me here, in this moment be at my side, to light and guard, to rule and guide!" As the first words came out of her mouth, the glowing angelic beings flew into action with such joy—as if they had been waiting all their lives for this moment—to be enlisted.

Clare felt a warm gust of wind.

She and her angels were an army, sure to win this battle.

Clare opened her eyes and continued to pray, "Lord have mercy, Christ have mercy, Lord have mercy." Both demons were screeching in horror.

They shielded their faces with their gnarled, arthritic hands.

Clare ran to her desk. There in the bottom drawer, she shoved through her collection of hair bands and lip gloss and pulled out some beads.

But these weren't just any beads. These were rosary beads—small, smooth stones arranged in a circle of love around the life, death, and resurrection of Jesus.

She clutched them in her hand and just as the angel Gabriel had greeted the future Mother of God, she began, "Hail Mary, full of grace, the Lord is with you. Blessed are you among women, and blessed is the fruit of your womb, Jesus."

She continued her petition, asking that Mary pray to Our Lord and Savior, Jesus, on her behalf, "Holy Mary, Mother of God, pray for us, sinners, now and at the hour of our death, Amen. In the name of Jesus Christ, I command you demons, be gone!"

The angels moved in tandem to the right and left, between Clare and the demons. The greatness of their beauty and goodness obstructed her view of the darkness on the other side.

She closed her eyes and continued to pray aloud, "Oh Lord, lead us not into temptation, and deliver us from evil. Jesus, I trust in you. Jesus, I trust in you. Jesus, I trust in you."

The open window sucked outwardly as if in a vacuum—the angry vaporous forms expelled with it—leaving only the heated glow of the angels in its wake.

Peace filled the room.

Peace filled Clare's heart.

Her soul was filled to the brim with unspeakable joy. It was the kind of joy that made one's skin tingle and occurred with the feeling of wanting to sing, laugh, and throw up all at the same time.

She dropped to her knees next to her bed.

Her eyes were on her angels, who had returned to their former positions in the corner of her bedroom. But something about them was different. If she had to name it, she would say they appeared to be inflamed with love, blazing even brighter than before. She could feel their joy—their satisfaction.

She realized they had probably been waiting years to serve her on behalf of her Glorious Savior.

The full greatness of her power in the Lord hit her. Even the angels of heaven were placed on earth for her—to serve *her*.

She is no *'mere mortal.'*

She is a daughter of the King!

Shaken but full of peace, Clare reached under her bed and pulled out a smooth wooden box. She unlatched it and ran her hand across the white, leather-bound book before taking it out. She picked it up and traced the engraved golden letters with her finger. The letters read, 'Clare Marie.' It was the Bible that was given to her at her First Communion.

There, at her bedside, she genuinely sought the Face of Jesus for the first time. She gently set the book on her purple, hand-sewn comforter and opened it to where the pale ribbon was already positioned. It was Philippians 4:6-7, and it read, "Have no anxiety at all, but in everything, by prayer and petition, with thanksgiving, make your requests known to God. Then the peace of God that surpasses all understanding will guard your hearts and minds in Christ Jesus."

As she knelt in prayer before the Lord, she opened her heart to the Holy Spirit and declared her faith, **"My Lord, my God, I desire a relationship with you. I know I can't save myself because I am a sinner. Thank you for dying on the cross for my sins. I believe you died for me, and I receive your free gift of salvation. I fully surrender my life to you. Help me change my ways and follow you all the days of my life. In Jesus' name, I pray. Amen."**

"If then you were raised with Christ, seek what is above, where Christ is seated at the right hand of God. Think of what is above, not of what is on earth."
Colossians 3:1-2

15

Reparation

When Clare woke, she felt relaxed. As the alarm blared to wake her up, she was still entirely at peace.

She felt grateful in a way she had never before felt. Though the previous week had been filled with horrors, she knew that this day was another chance. She had made a life-altering choice.

She had surrendered to God.

And although she used to think that surrendering her life would make her a slave, she now realized that this type of surrender meant true freedom. Freedom from her sin.

Freedom from her old ways. Freedom to be fully alive in Christ who makes all things new.

As she washed her face and tidied her hair, she didn't gaze at herself with criticism but instead closed her eyes in front of the mirror and prayed that she would see herself as God sees her, with grace and mercy. She opened her eyes and accepted herself for who her Creator designed her to be. Her auburn hair no longer seemed dull but now reflected the hue of the changing leaves outside her bedroom window—her green eyes the color of new spring grass.

Clare opened her closet. Dressing for the school day didn't mean the same thing that it used to. It was no longer a tool to get her attention or a status symbol. Her body was no longer a billboard for Nike, Under Armour, or Puma. No. Today she would cloth herself in dignity, as the temple of God she was.

She chose a white sweater with oversized burgundy roses that cascaded across the soft flowing fabric from the front to the back.

As she joined her family in the kitchen this day, their chatter wasn't an annoyance but a reminder of how blessed she was to have people she loved beside her. She recalled Noah's words in front of his mother's grave that night in the cemetery, "none of us get out alive," and was reminded to be grateful for each moment.

Riding her bike to school was an experience of joy. The cooling October wind bit at her, but it felt more like sparks today. What her mother had said to her had been true; a spark can grow into a flame if we allow it. Clare seemed to hear the chirp of the birds with new clarity, and the cool wind in her hair enlivened her soul.

As she walked up to the school, she saw Noah standing off to the side with some of his friends.

He paused and looked up at her as she passed. "Wow. You look beautiful today."

"Thank you," she said, grinning.

There was a new confidence in her.

A new light.

She walked ahead into the comparative darkness of the building's interior.

Although Clare was different today, the school atmosphere remained unchanged. Colton and Finn were down at the other end of the hall, throwing a football back and forth as the principal shouted for them to 'stop their shenanigans and get to class.'

For the first few periods of the day, Clare felt the vibrancy of her newfound faith. It propelled her forward with boldness. But now, as history class came closer, she became aware of a growing desire inside her. A desire for justice. A desire for revenge.

She entered the History classroom and took her seat, directly in front of Noah. She stared at the back of Nikki's blond head two rows ahead of her as she began to imagine how the next fifty minutes would play out.

Clare knew she had a choice to make. Would she go ahead and present her report—a story that would 'out' Nikki and her family, for good? Or would she choose the higher road? Could she forgive Nikki? She wasn't sure.

She knew it would be her turn to present a report soon, and her nerves were building.

Whatever choice she made, it likely wouldn't gain her popularity with someone—whether that someone was her teacher for failing to fulfill the essay requirements or Nikki for throwing her under the bus of social damnation.

It all came down to this.

"Clare Thomson," Mr. Schwab's voice rang out.

Clare stood up, brushed off her pants, and straightened her sweater. She picked up the essay she had written the night before and tapped the three pages on her desk to align them before approaching the front of the class.

She felt everyone's eyes on her. As much as she hated speaking in front of people, this was the moment she had been waiting for. The words on these pages would reveal to the entire class—and eventually the entire school—that Nikki Thacker and her family were nothing but a bunch of lying, cheating, thieving criminals—that they were responsible for the economic downfall of the town and even the death of an innocent woman.

She pictured Nikki's red, horrified face as she would jump up from her desk and run, bawling, to the bathroom.

Oh, the vindication.

Oh, the justice.

She looked over at Noah. His eyes were locked on hers. He was mouthing something. What was it? He mouthed it again. She made out the words, "forgive us our trespasses, as we forgive those who trespass against us."

She knew those words. And not only that, she knew the meaning behind them.

Just as she had been forgiven by God, she was called to forgive others—even Nikki Thacker.

She glanced at Nikki, who was turned, talking to the girl next to her. There she was grinning her contemptuous little grin, chewing the gum she was always chewing, whispering the slanderous, hurtful words she was always whispering.

"Miss Thacker!" the teacher's voice rang out. "Do you have something to share with the class?"

"Nah, Mr. Schwab," Nikki responded, still grinning. She turned around to glare at Clare.

"Miss Thomson," his voice boomed again. "Please begin." He sat down at his desk and nodded in Clare's direction.

Clare took a deep breath.

"I'm sorry, Mr. Schwab. I wasn't able to finish the assignment." She glanced from her teacher to Noah, who now relaxed in his seat. A calm but pleased expression was on his face.

"Clare, this is unacceptable," Mr. Schwab began. "You do understand that you will receive a zero for this assignment?" he asked, peering over his reading glasses, pen in hand.

"I understand, sir," Clare replied, taking a seat.

"You did the right thing," Noah whispered as she returned to her seat.

"I hope so," she replied, more to herself than to him. She glanced over at Caitlin, who had been avoiding eye contact with her since she came into the room. It was her turn next.

Caitlin stood up. She presented to the class a detailed account of the progression of the logging industry over its 100-year history in Newhill. As she finished, the class clapped for her. Mr. Schwab thanked her, and she took her seat.

After a hilarious slideshow from a boy named Clark, who read his report while displaying a slideshow of headshots of each of the town's 32 mayors amusingly filtered to look like Snapchat cats, it was Noah's turn.

He walked to the front of the room and presented a well-written report on hydro-power and its use in the paper industry. He finished, gave Clare a knowing look, and took his seat.

After class, all of the students filtered out into the hall. Clare reached toward Caitlin, hoping to get her attention—hoping to apologize—but Caitlin slipped out before she had the chance.

As Clare made her way to her locker, she wondered if she had done the right thing. Had she missed her chance to get even—her last chance to give Nikki the justice that she deserved?

As she was wondering this, she felt fingers slide between hers. It was Noah. He smiled down at her. She looked up into his deep brown eyes and then down at their hands, entwined. She took his other hand and smiled back.

"Well, look at these two love birds," Nikki said as she aligned herself with Clare, Colton at her side, football in hand. "Finally made a move, huh, Clare Bear. Honestly, you two are perfect for each other. Look at you. You make me sick. What are you wearing anyway? Did you rob your grandma's closet?"

"C'mon, Nik. Just leave her alone," Elise interjected.

"What?! You too, now?! You've got to be kidding me! Everyone around here is getting soft. Look at her! She's a joke!" Nikki gestured her hand at Clare's modest attire.

Elise turned and walked a few paces away.

"Ya know, Nikki," Clare began. "I'm sorry."

"What?" Nikki snarled.

"I'm sorry that you don't know peace. I'm sorry that you hate yourself so much that you have to knock others down so that they are so small that you feel big. But most of all, I'm sorry that you don't know Love."

Nikki said nothing but just scrunched her nose in response. Her attention then shifted to who was coming down the hall. It was Caitlin. She was on her way to her next class carrying a giant mock-up of the solar system. Her brown eyes were peering between the orbital foam and glitter as she navigated her way through the jungle of students.

She just about made it to the science lab before Nikki laughed, glaring from Clare to Caitlin and back again. She called out, "Elise! Get your phone! This is gonna be good!" She then took the football out of Colton's hands and said to him, winking, "Hey, Colt, go long."

Colton took off at a run towards Caitlin and her teetering model.

"No!" Clare yelled as she dove, and just like you see in the NFL, Clare took Nikki out at the knees, just as the ball released from her hand. But instead of sending it flying in Cait's direction, she instead sent it soaring, hitting Mr. Schwab squarely in the jaw just as he turned to see what all of the commotion was about.

He adjusted his glasses and had fire in his eyes while he rubbed his face and shouted, "Nikki Thacker! DETENTION!"

And, it seemed, for the first time in her life, Nikki was speechless.

Clare stood up and walked to Caitlin, who was standing in apparent shock and awe. Then Clare took one side of the gigantic model, and together, they carried it down the hall to safety.

Noah followed close behind, beaming with pride.

Elise did capture the moment that fateful day, and she even managed to pass it on to most of the school before Nikki forced her to delete it from her phone.

After that, Clare and Caitlin were no longer Nikki's favorite chew toys, and after a sincere apology for leaving Caitlin in the dust back at the mill, Caitlin forgave Clare wholeheartedly.

"Finally, brothers, whatever is true, whatever is honorable, whatever is just, whatever is pure, whatever is lovely, whatever is gracious, if there is any excellence and if there is anything worthy of praise, think about these things. Keep on doing what you have learned and received and heard and seen in me. Then the God of peace will be with you."
Philippians 4:8-9

16
Renewal

Eight months had passed since had Clare picked up the sunglasses out of the mill yard that dark night.

It was now a glorious spring Sunday. Birds were chirping, and the sun was shining. Clare stood outside St. Anne's after Mass with her family, her skin warm in the sun. James was running around the legs of parishioners, taunting Clare to a game of tag. She humored him, laughing as she chased her little brother in circles across the lawn in front of the church.

Noah was walking across the parking lot with his father and sister. When he noticed Clare in the yard he jogged over, picked her up, and swung her in a circle before letting her feet gently touch back to the ground.

They smiled at each other and held hands then strolled to join Clare's family near the church's doors.

"Sir, would it be all right with you if I walk Clare home?" Noah asked Clare's father.

"Ya know, sport, that's a three-mile walk."

"I don't mind. It will be the best three miles of my day." Noah smiled thoughtfully at Clare.

"All right. Don't forget to stop for ice cream," Mr. Thomson replied as he handed Noah a ten-dollar bill.

"Thanks, Dad." Clare hugged her father tightly, without reserve. Then she took Noah's hand and they strolled along the sidewalk. The sunglasses hung from the front of her flowing floral top. "Do you mind if we stop to see Ethan." She gestured towards the cemetery.

"Of course not," he replied.

They walked towards the gate, stopping to pick some small purple-and-yellow flowers that were growing from the cracks along the curb.

They stood side-by-side in front of Ethan's granite headstone which glinted in the morning sun. Clare stooped to set the flowers in front of it then stood and put the sunglasses on to admire the angel she already knew was there.

As she did this, she took Noah's hand in hers. "When someone you love dies, it feels as though time stops; the world as you have always known it has ended. For the longest time, I thought that my world was over because it no longer was the way it used to be. But, now I see. I see that we're not here to remain the same."

She paused, breathing in deep the fresh spring air. "I'm ready now."

"Ready for what, Clare?" Noah asked, gazing down at her.

" 'Blessed are those who have not seen and have believed.' ...I don't think I need these

248

anymore." She removed the sunglasses from her face, dangling them from her fingertips.

Noah squeezed her hand as he said, "For we walk by faith, not by sight."

Clare paused. "Maybe they could do for someone else what they've done for me." Then she bent and carefully placed the glasses on Ethan's grave. Noah pulled her close and gently kissed her forehead. Then they turned and walked together along the long gravel path into the ever-rising sun.

If only they had known, in the shadows lurked someone whose name they already knew—all too well.

ENLIST YOUR GUARDIAN ANGEL IN THE SPIRITUAL BATTLE TODAY!

"ANGEL OF GOD,
MY GUARDIAN DEAR,
TO WHOM GOD'S LOVE,
COMMITS ME HERE,

EVER THIS NIGHT/DAY,
BE AT MY SIDE,
TO LIGHT AND GUARD,
TO RULE AND GUIDE.

AMEN.

Don't miss Book 2 of The HIDDEN Series!

SECRETS:
The Truth Will Out
Elise's Story
(A Pro-life Novel)

Have you ever heard that 'the truth will set you free?' High schooler Elise Thames could hardly agree. When she's gifted a bracelet that gives her a vision into the minds of others, her identity as one of the most popular girls in the school is shaken. And when an unplanned pregnancy exposes the cracks in every relationship she's ever depended on, Elise must face the truth about who she is—and make a choice.

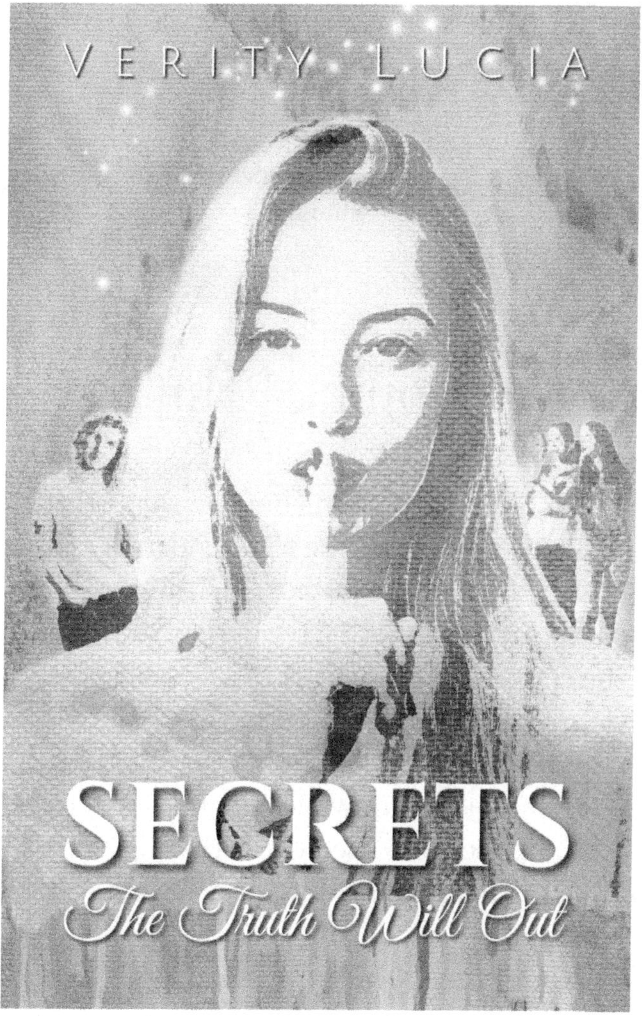
VERITY LUCIA
SECRETS
The Truth Will Out

Here's a sneak peek of Book 2!
SECRETS: The Truth Will Out

"In this world you will have trouble. But take heart!
I have overcome the world."
- John 16:33

1

Tipping Point

Elise stood, facing into the wind. Her naked heels lifted off the frigid concrete balcony floor as she pushed up with her hands on the icy railing. From twenty-six stories up, she could see miles across the crystalline October waters of Lake Michigan.   Her eyes searched the sky for stars, but the harsh city lights of Chicago drowned out any hint of them. She could see only the ever-darkening blue ombre of the rippling waves reaching out before her.

No shore in sight.

Too numb to feel the cutting gusts that bit her bare toes and perfectly polished fingertips, Elise sensed only the melting despair in the void of her soul as her toes suspended from the floor.

LIVE THE MESSAGE

Keep the spiritual battle at the forefront of your mind!

Connect with me, Verity Lucia, at
<u>VerityLuciaBooks.com</u>
Subscribe to my newsletter
for a *FREE* giveaway.

Instagram | Goodreads | Facebook

Don't forget to <u>visit my website</u> for a
FREE Conversation Starter Worksheet.
Read along with your teen to get the most out of
HIDDEN and expand your understanding of the
Catholic faith, together!

Lead them to TRUTH through the excitement of fiction!

With the purchase of this book you receive a complimentary eBook.
Scan this code to download your free copy.

Did you enjoy this book?

If so, please **consider sharing it with others.** It
is up to generous readers like you to
**help the message of God's loving mercy reach
those who need it most.**

Please leave a review at www.amazon.com.
Every review helps this book reach another
potential reader.

✝

For more information about Catholicism visit
www.Catholic.com or if you are in need of
resources please visit a Catholic church near you.

**Thank you!
Please know that all readers are in my prayers
daily.**

Love and prayers,
Verily Lucia

GLOSSARY

Angel: Translated from Hebrew meaning 'Messenger.' Angels are purely spiritual beings created by God to glorify Him forever in heaven and intermediate between God and men. Angels, being purely spiritual beings, do not have physical bodies. However, they are said to appear in differing forms depending on their purpose. Note: Angels are distinct from humans. Humans do not become angels upon death and entrance into heaven. At that point, the person would be referred to as a 'saint.'

Bible: A divinely inspired work made of two distinct collections (The Old Testament and The New Testament) compiled by many faithful early Christians. The Bible was first made available in mass production in 1455 by Johann Gutenberg.

Catholic: Translated 'Universal.'
Catholic Church = Universal Church.

Demon: An angel which rejected God and now dwells in hell and/or on earth. Otherwise referred to as a fallen angel or devil.

Grace: God's life.

Holy: Blessed/sacred/set apart.

Homily: A commentary given by a priest or deacon following a reading of sacred scripture often intended to inform the congregation in an insightful way about Church doctrine and its relation to our lives today.

Love: To will the good of the other. Or an act of sacrificial charity. Love can be a feeling, but it is ultimately an act in which we desire good for someone. Note: One can love without 'feeling loving.' Also, God is Love.

Mass: The ultimate prayer and form of worship where Our Lord's sacrifice of His body and blood on the cross is made present to us again. During the Mass, we are united as followers of Christ in a shared meal, giving glory to God and heaven. Alongside the angels, we receive Jesus Christ fully in the Eucharist by which we are given Grace and strength to live out our vocations here on earth.

Prayer: The act of lifting our hearts and minds to God. This sometimes takes the form of a petition. It is sometimes in thanks. It is sometimes with words. And sometimes without.

Rosary: A biblical prayer during which one meditates on the life, death, and resurrection of Jesus Christ while asking Mary, the Mother of God, to pray to her son on your behalf.

Sacrament: A sacred sign instituted by Jesus Christ to give Grace. (ie. Baptism, Confirmation, Holy Orders, Reconciliation, Holy Matrimony, Anointing of the Sick and Holy Communion.

Saint: Someone in heaven.

The Church: The society founded by Jesus Christ in his final days on earth. Also known as the Bride of Christ. She is ultimately a body of believers who strive to do God's will on earth.

RESOURCES

I highly recommend the following books and websites. They are invaluable resources in the search for truth and meaning, which is found in full within the Catholic Faith.

The Holy Bible (I highly recommend the Great Adventure Catholic Bible *Available for purchase at www.ascensionpress.com*)

The Catechism of the Catholic Church, Second Edition, Doubleday, (*Available for purchase at www.ignatius.com*)

John Burke, *Imagine Heaven - Near-Death Experiences. God's Promises, and the Exhilarating Future That Awaits You*, Copyright 2015 John Burke, (*Available for purchase at www.imagineheaven.net*)

Fr. Jose Antonio Fortea, *Interview with an Exorcist*, Copyright 2006 Ascension Press, LLC, (*Available for purchase at www.ascensionpress.com*)

Peter Kreeft, *Angels (and Demons) What Do We Really Know About Them*, Copyright 1995 Peter J. Kreeft, (*Available for purchase at www.ignatius.com*)

www.Catholic.com

CITATIONS

[1] Fr. Jose Antonio Fortea, *Interview with an Exorcist*, pg. 58

[2] Peter Kreeft, *Angels (and Demons) What Do We Really Know About Them*, pg. 86

[3] Fr. Jose Antonio Fortea, *Interview with an Exorcist*, pg. 25

THANKS

First, I would like to thank my Savior Jesus Christ, without whom I would not have been able to breathe life into this story. To God be the glory, always and forever, Amen.

Also, thank you to my mother, who had to listen to me work through plot points again and again. You are always so supportive! I love you more!

To my husband, who allowed me to work late nights and never doubted my reasons.

And to all those who participated in the production and launch of this publication: Maria, Birgitta, Sophia, and especially my blessed editor and formatter, Ellen Gable. I couldn't do it without you!

ABOUT THE AUTHOR

Catholic Christian Author Verity Lucia is a former catechist for teens, a wife, and a mom of four. She is an architectural designer by trade but began writing to speak into the hearts of her children about the challenges of living in a broken world. What started as a way to talk with her daughter about the difficulties of being a teen has become a book series that she hopes will enhance how we teach the Catholic Faith to our youth.

Made in the USA
Monee, IL
07 September 2023

42233616R00156